"What's your passion?" Sara asked.

Family. Cade longed for a circle of loved ones gathered around him. He wanted the hugs and tears, the teasing, the laughter, even the disagreements that happened between people who had confidence that no matter what, the ones who mattered would always be there for him.

His worst fear was that his sister would marry and want to live somewhere other than the ranch. That his dream of a family nearby would die. But as he smiled into Sara's wide, glowing eyes, Cade knew he couldn't say it. She wouldn't understand why family was so important to him, not without hearing a lot of back history.

She was smiling at him. "I should warn you, Cade, that some of my ideas for wedding planning are usually, er, off the wall."

He tucked a ringlet behind her ear. "It's the off-the-wall ideas that usually turn out best, Sara Woodward," he told her quietly.

Books by Lois Richer

Love Inspired

A Will and a Wedding	*Inner Harbor*
*Faithfully Yours	†Blessings
*A Hopeful Heart	†Heaven's Kiss
*Sweet Charity	†A Time to Remember
A Home, a Heart, a Husband	Past Secrets, Present Love
This Child of Mine	‡‡His Winter Rose
**Baby on the Way	‡‡Apple Blossom Bride
**Daddy on the Way	‡‡Spring Flowers, Summer Love
**Wedding on the Way	§Healing Tides
‡Mother's Day Miracle	§Heart's Haven
‡His Answered Prayer	§A Cowboy's Honor
‡Blessed Baby	§§Rocky Mountain Legacy
Tucker's Bride	

Love Inspired Suspense

A Time To Protect	*Faith, Hope & Charity
††Secrets of the Rose	**Brides of the Seasons
††Silent Enemy	‡If Wishes Were Weddings
††Identity: Undercover	†Blessings in Disguise
	††Finders Inc.
	‡‡Serenity Bay
	§Pennies from Heaven
	§§Weddings By Woodwards

LOIS RICHER

Lois Richer likes variety. From her time in human resources management to entrepreneurship, life has held plenty of surprises.

She says, "Having given up on fairy tales, I was happily involved in building a restaurant when a handsome prince walked into my life and upset all my career plans with a wedding ring. Motherhood quickly followed. I guess the seeds of my storytelling took root because of two small boys who kept demanding 'Then what, Mom?'"

The miracle of God's love for His children, the blessing of true love, the joy of sharing Him with others—that is a story that can be told a thousand ways and yet still be brand-new. Lois Richer intends to go right on telling it.

Rocky Mountain Legacy
Lois Richer

Steeple Hill®

Published by Steeple Hill Books™

STEEPLE HILL BOOKS

Steeple Hill®

Recycling programs
for this product may
not exist in your area.

ISBN-13: 978-0-373-87511-5
ISBN-10:   0-373-87511-8

ROCKY MOUNTAIN LEGACY

Copyright © 2009 by Lois M. Richer

www.SteepleHill.com

Printed in U.S.A.

For I am persuaded beyond doubt that neither death, nor life, nor angels, nor principalities, nor things impending and threatening, nor things to come, nor powers, nor height, nor depth, nor anything else in all creation, will be able to separate us from the love of God which is in Christ Jesus our Lord.
—*Romans* 8:38–39

Chapter One

"Catch us, Auntie Sara!"

Giggles overrode romantic flute music flowing from overhead speakers as Sara Woodward reached for, and missed, her two squirming nephews. Brett and Brady slipped past her and through a narrow door that led into the display windows of Weddings by Woodwards bridal shop.

A door Sara had left ajar.

"You're not allowed in here, guys," she whispered. She followed only after she'd checked to be sure none of the family was nearby. "Come out of there right now."

But the mischievous pair would not emerge, and their impromptu game of tag was wreaking havoc with her grandmother's bridal displays. Italian silk wasn't meant for three-year-old boys with dirty sneakers.

Sara tried negotiation, to no avail.

Now what?

"If those two are someone's ring bearers, you'll have your hands full getting them down the aisle."

Startled by the masculine voice behind her, Sara yelped and jerked upright. The back of her head bumped the arm of a groom mannequin, dislodging its top hat and cane. The brass-tipped ebony stick pinged against the display window with a clatter.

It seemed the entire building fell silent, including the two causes of this mayhem. Brady's face wrinkled. He was going to start crying. Judging by the droop of his twin's bottom lip, Brett wouldn't be far behind.

Sara knew exactly how they felt. Nothing about today was going right.

"Sorry I scared you." Amusement laced the man's voice the way a drop of rich cream mellows coffee. "Maybe I can help. Grab the one in blue and pass him to me, then you can haul out the red-shirted one. Okay?"

"I'll try. Thanks." Sara didn't dare take her eyes off the twins. "Come on, Brett. Out you go."

"No." It was his favorite word.

Sara desperately wished she'd been late this morning and therefore unavailable to watch her brother's kids while he took an important call. Coming home to help out the family was one thing, but babysitting in a bridal store was asking for trouble.

A wicker basket hit the floor, scattering rose petals everywhere.

"Come on, Brett. We'll play with your toys," she wheedled.

"No."

"No," Brady copied.

"Auntie will get you a new toy." Sara clung to her smile, feeling a fool in front of the stranger. Ordinarily she deplored bribery, but this situation called for desperate measures. "Don't you want a new toy?"

"No."

"Yes!" Exasperated, Sara extended her fingertips to snag a belt loop on Brett's tiny blue jeans just as the voice behind her inquired:

"I don't suppose either of them likes candy?"

"Candy?" Brett surged up so fast his head hit Sara's chin, knocking her teeth together. He dropped the tulle he'd pulled down, almost forcing her off balance as he launched himself through the narrow passage. "I like candy. Candy's good."

"Sometimes it's very good." The voice behind Sara sounded amused by the bundle of nonstop energy. "Gotcha. But we can't have candy without your brother. Can you sit very still and wait for him?"

"Brett's a good boy."

"You sure are," the visitor agreed. "I wonder how good your brother is."

The man knew kids. Brady's frown deepened. He glared at Sara as if she'd maligned his character. Or tried to steal his treat.

"Brady's good, too!" He dropped to all fours, crawled between Sara's feet and out the door.

"Got him, too," the masculine voice triumphed. "You can come out now."

Sara wasn't sure she wanted to. Not if it meant another half hour of trying to pry grimy fingers off the pristine bridal dresses displayed all over the foyer.

"I assure you, it's safe." Laughter colored the edge of their visitor's low-throated rumble. "For now, anyway."

"I'm coming." She rubbed one finger against her throbbing skull and found her way blocked. "Would you step back? It's very narrow here."

"Sure is." He jostled the door against a tulle-covered arch laced with nodding sunflowers. The arch jiggled, then shifted. That knocked off the bride's arm. It clattered to the floor along with her bouquet of dried autumn wildflowers.

The resulting mess was a far cry from Woodward's usually chichi displays, but fixing it now was out of the question. Sara could only hope she'd get time to rectify matters before the family noticed.

Dream on. When had the family not noticed anything that affected Weddings by Woodwards?

"Something wrong? Need help?"

"I can manage."

There was no point wishing their visitor wouldn't witness her backward, very uncool duckwalk out of the passage. Free at last, Sara clicked the lock closed, frustrated and fed up with the way her life wasn't going.

"Winifred Woodward?"

Did she look almost eighty?

"No." Sara bent to straighten her black skirt, buying time to regain the composure Denver's hottest wedding store and its employees were known for. "But if you need help with a wedding, you're in the right place. Weddings by Woodwards takes pride in planning weddings that are unique to every bride and groom we serve."

The stock phrase slipped easily to her lips. Good thing, because when Sara glanced up at the owner of that coffee-and-cream voice, her throat jammed closed.

"Kidding." He winked at her. "I was kidding. I could tell when I walked past the windows that you aren't Mrs. Woodward."

Meaning he knew her grandmother?

Sara took stock of her visitor. Slightly older than the usual Woodwards' groom, he stood nearly six feet tall. The mass of unruly mahogany curls cut close against his scalp could have given him a rakish look—except for the plump baby fingers threading through them.

"I'll take him." She reached out for Brady who glared at her and clutched his rescuer all the tighter. "Or not."

"He's fine." The visitor wore black tooled-leather boots,

fitted jeans and a battered leather jacket that almost screamed "wild west." Evidently her nephew thought the same.

"Cowboy," Brady said, trailing his grubby paws against the leather. "Horsie?"

"Not here, pal." The man chuckled as he tousled Brady's hair. "But I have some at home on my ranch."

"Horsies are good. Candy's good."

Sara's rescuer burst into deep-throated laughter that filled the two-story foyer.

"Not very subtle, are you, son?"

This cowboy was movie-star material. Substitute his leather and jeans for a wedding tux, and any bride would race down the aisle. On closer scrutiny, Sara glimpsed an indefinable quality to those blue eyes that branded this man as more substantial than a mere movie star. The twins recognized it, too, because they remained perfectly still, staring at him.

"Thank you for helping. They're a bit of a handful."

"I can imagine." His face was all sharp angles. Etched lines carved out the corners of his eyes, as if he'd known sadness and grief too often. His sapphire stare captivated Sara, pushed past her barriers and peered inside, as if to expose the secrets she kept hidden from the world.

Or maybe it was all in her mind.

"I have an appointment to speak with Winifred Woodward." He eased Brady's grip from his hair and lowered the boy so his feet rested on the floor. "There you go, buddy."

An icon in the wedding-planning business, Grandma Winnie was always fielding so-called appointments of people who simply wanted to meet the matriarch of Weddings by Woodwards. Winnie, sweet woman that she was, would never refuse them. That's why Sara had come home.

Recent exhaustion had lowered Winnie's ability to fight a cold and, according to the family, her grandmother needed complete rest to recover. Sara's job was to fill in wherever she was needed at Woodwards.

Today that meant manning the reception desk.

And babysitting.

"Your name?"

"Cade Porter."

"You weren't in her appointment book, Mr. Porter." Sara knew because she'd canceled or rebooked all Winnie's appointments last week, the day after she'd returned to Denver.

"Nevertheless, I do have an appointment." Dark brows climbed, daring her to dispute it. "Would you direct me to her office please?"

"I'm afraid that isn't going to be possible."

The eyebrows elevated a millimeter higher. Jutting cheekbones and a forceful chin told Sara that Cade Porter wouldn't give up easily.

"Candy?" Brady reminded.

"You have to wait a moment, sweetie."

"'Kay."

"Good boy." Sara savored his winsome smile before returning to her customer. "I'm assuming you're here to talk about planning a wedding, Mr. Porter. If you can wait, I'll find you a planner as soon as I get these two settled. I have to watch them until my brother returns. As you've noticed, they take a lot of watching."

"I did notice." Cade Porter's lips lifted in a grin. He squatted down and spoke quietly to the twins, showing them two wrapped peppermints, identical to the ones filling a crystal bowl on the counter. He glanced at her belatedly. "Okay with you?"

She nodded.

"Anything to keep them busy." She ignored the inner warning that said sugar wasn't the best choice. One candy couldn't hurt.

"Here are the rules, guys." Mr. Porter waited until their attention was focused on him. "You have to sit here until you're finished. Then we'll wash your hands. After that, maybe I'll tell you about my horses. Is it a deal?"

Enthralled, the twins nodded, received their candy and began unwrapping. Mr. Porter rose. His face lost the soft amusement as he studied Sara.

"Look, I'm sure you employ good people here, but I want Mrs. Woodward. I confirmed with her eight days ago. Surely Weddings by Woodwards doesn't promise their clients one thing and then…"

Sara might not want to be part of the family business, but nobody disparaged it and got away unchallenged.

"My grandmother was taken ill a week ago. I regret that you weren't informed." She bent to pick up the wrappers the boys had tossed on the pale pink carpet. "And I'm very sorry that you've been inconvenienced. But because Winnie won't be back at work for at least a month, I'm afraid you'll have to make a new appointment. Or accept help from someone else."

His heavily lashed eyes darkened.

"I'm sorry she's ill. Maybe—" He stopped, frowned as if reconsidering.

Red flags soared in Sara's brain. If she lost a potential client, her sister Katie would be on her case all afternoon.

"If you'll—" Sara almost choked when Brett's sticky fingers grabbed Mr. Porter at the knee. She eased Brady's hand away. What was taking Reese so long? "I'm sorry about that," she apologized, trying to recall who might be free to deal with Mr. Porter.

"They're just jeans. They won't melt. Can you get a wet cloth?"

"A cloth?" His generous smile confused her usually functioning brain.

"To wipe off the kids. I don't think those pretty dresses on display will look quite as nice with peppermint smeared all over them." He brushed Brady's hair with a big capable hand. "We'll get this pair busy drawing a horse. Then maybe you and I can get started."

Sara frowned. Started—doing what?

"Cloth?" he reminded her as he kept Brett's hand from touching a length of veiling.

"Right." She fetched a damp washcloth and tried to wipe Brett's fingers, but her nephew veered away, clinging to Mr. Porter.

"Let me." He took the cloth and with gentle thoroughness wiped down two faces and four hands, teasing the boys as he did. Her nephews had never behaved so well.

"Don't look so surprised. Kids usually like me." Mr. Porter grinned as he handed back the cloth.

"I'm sure they do. I've just never seen these two so quiet." Sara got rid of the sticky cloth. "Except maybe when they're asleep."

Mr. Porter's lips twitched. He hunkered down next to the boys who were arguing over the crayons and paper pads scattered across the coffee table. He told them a little about his ranch, then promised a special treat for whoever could draw the best horse.

How did he know competition was the best way to get them focused?

"Okay, now can we talk about my wedding?" Cade Porter rose, folded his arms across his wide chest, charm oozing from the lopsided smile he flashed at her. "Unless Woodward Weddings can't handle it."

"Weddings by Woodwards," she corrected.

"Yeah, that." His gaze slid to the wall above the counter. "I assume that array of diplomas includes you as one of the wedding planners?"

Sara followed his gaze, noticed a silver framed certificate

she'd earned four years ago hanging among the rest of the family's. Trust her sister to dig it out and display it, as if Sara was permanently back on staff.

"I—um—"

"My mistake." His mouth tightened. "I'd prefer Mrs. Woodward to handle things, but because that's out, perhaps you'll summon whoever's handling her cases."

Offended, Sara bristled to her own defense.

"I *am* a certified wedding planner, Mr. Porter. I've planned about forty weddings and I am quite capable of handling your needs." Even if her family always interfered.

"I need someone who can deal with the unusual." He studied her for several moments, his gaze dark and inscrutable.

"Then you need me." The words slipped out without a second thought. Sara almost groaned. She was as bad as the twins, taking the bait faster than they'd latched on to his promise of candy.

"Do I?" Cade Porter blinked.

His dubious demeanor underscored her own growing doubts. Like her siblings, Sara had begun learning about the wedding business shortly after she learned to walk. But she hadn't planned a wedding since she'd walked out of Weddings by Woodwards two years ago to escape her loving, but constantly meddling family.

Which did not mean she'd forgotten everything she'd learned here.

"What kind of a wedding do you want, Mr. Porter?"

"That's an odd question." He scratched his shaven chin, seemingly stymied. "How many kinds are there?"

"Many." Obviously Cade Porter was a complete innocent.

"Horsie." Brett held up his scribble.

"Hmm. Not bad. But he needs legs."

While Cade and the boys discussed horse anatomy, Sara

found a notepad and pen. She'd come home to help. Might as well do her best.

"What are my choices?" he asked, twisting his head to study her.

"When are you to be married?"

"I'm not." He frowned at her. "It's not *my* wedding."

"So you're *not* getting married—but you want to plan a wedding?" Sara's headache amplified.

"Exactly." Humor twinkled in the depths of his blue eyes. "I want to plan a wedding for my sister."

"Ah." While her brother Reese probably wouldn't plan a wedding for her, Sara was pretty sure the rest of the family certainly would. They'd find her a groom, arrange the ceremony and take over every detail without asking for her input—if she let them.

Sara loved her family dearly, but they refused to acknowledge that she was an adult who could think and choose her own course in life.

"Those two tornadoes aren't going to color for long," Cade reminded.

"Sorry. I was thinking." She had to find out about Mr. Porter's sister. Having experienced prying too often herself, Sara decided on tact. "Weddings should be personal. If your sister prefers an outdoor location, spring or summer events work best. Is she thinking of a large event? Sit-down reception? Church wedding or—"

"Yes!"

"Yes?" Pulling teeth would be easier. "Yes—what, exactly?"

"Church wedding. I think." He glanced around the reception area. His nose wrinkled when his glance landed on delicate white wrought iron chairs with their tufted white silk cushions. "The reception can't be stuffy. Not like—"

Mr. Porter cut himself off, but the glare he shot toward tiny

Victorian chairs her grandmother favored made Sara smile. Tact indeed.

"Not stuffy—like this. Is that what you mean?" she asked, tongue in cheek.

"Well…yes." He shied away from meeting her stare.

"I see. It would be helpful for the bride to be present for her wedding plans." That wasn't being nosy. "If your sister could—"

"She can't. You'll have to manage with me. Unless…"

He let his voice trail away, but Sara got the message. Unless she had a problem. And Weddings by Woodwards did not have problems with clients.

Ever.

"Perhaps something less—er," Cade Porter's aquiline nose twitched as he glanced at the very girlish frilly bridal gown on the main pedestal display.

"I understand." Sara swallowed her laughter. "Don't worry. We're not only about froufrou. We cater to many tastes." She checked the wall, scanned the work board. "To prove it, I'd show you a very masculine area, but at the moment it's being used by two men being fitted for tuxedos."

"Awkward." His lazy smile was a dentist's dream.

"Slightly. A tour of Weddings by Woodwards would illustrate the variety we offer. But I have to look after the boys and…"

"It doesn't matter." The look on his face said Cade Porter understood that none of the rooms would be suitable for Brett and Brady. "We'll go on to something else."

That was generous of him. Sara also noted how he praised both boys' drawings, then promised he'd choose a winner after they added a few more details.

"You're good with kids," she said when he straightened.

"I love them. Kids are amazing." Was that a hint of longing in his voice? "Families are so much fun."

Fun wasn't exactly how Sara would describe her relatives.

"Maybe *you* should tell *me* your ideas for this wedding." Sara waited. Seconds stretched to minutes of unbearable tension. She frowned. "You don't have any ideas?"

He shrugged. A hint of—embarrassment?—shadowed his eyes.

"My ideas include a minister, flowers, some music. I thought planning a wedding would be a simple matter of my telling you and you doing it." He glanced around the room. "Guess I was wrong."

"Horsie all done." Brady held up his picture in triumph.

"Good boy—"

"I was on the phone, and I heard a racket. You didn't let the boys ruin anything, did you, Sara?" Katie stepped through the back door, caught sight of their visitor and immediately thrust out one perfectly manicured hand. "I'm sorry to interrupt. You must be Mr. Porter."

"I am."

"Katie Woodward. I'm afraid I found a notation about your appointment with Winnie only a few moments ago. I tried to call, but you'd already left home."

Sara glanced at Cade, found his gaze on her. *See,* his eyes chided.

"More candy?" Brett asked hopefully, peering upward at the cowboy.

Cade turned his attention to the twins as he debated the winner of their coloring contest.

"Sara?" Katie hissed. "Problem?"

"Mr. Porter is interested in a church wedding. With the twins present, it's difficult for us to carry on a discussion. Perhaps you could help him while I babysit?" Keeping her back toward the man in question, Sara silently begged her sister to intervene.

"I'm booked with consults all day, sorry. But Reese will

be down in a few minutes. Apparently the agency is sending him a new nanny to replace the one who quit this morning. He'll take the twins when he goes to meet her." Katie leaned closer and whispered, "Is there some reason why you don't want to handle Mr. Porter's wedding?"

"Aside from the fact that I haven't done one in two years?"

"You'll do fine. Your weddings were always the most unique."

Sara made a face. During her previous employment at Woodwards, her family had meddled with every wedding plan she'd organized—just like they interfered in everything else in her life.

Which was why she'd left.

Reese chose that moment to thunder down the stairs, calling to his sons. He stopped when he saw Cade. Sara introduced the two men.

"Congratulations. You have two creative artists in the making." Cade showed him the pictures. "They're horses," he hinted as Reese tilted his head sideways.

"They're fantastic horses." Reese ruffled the boys' hair. "Good job, guys."

From his speculative look, Sara knew her brother was taking stock of their client. Reese had to notice the way his sons refused to release Cade's pant leg even after the cowboy awarded a tie for first place, but her brother made no effort to free their client.

"Brady, Brett, let go of Mr. Porter." Embarrassed, Sara tried to shift the chubby fingers, with no success. "I'm afraid they come by their stubbornness honestly," she apologized. "Reese was just as determined when we were kids."

"And so was I." He grinned at Reese. "Could I invite you and your boys for a horse ride at my ranch—in the interest of adding perspective to their artistic endeavors? And because they both won first prize?"

"Are you sure you want to do that?" Reese asked after shushing the boys' begging pleas. "How long have you had with them? Obviously not long enough to recognize the devastation they bring."

"I have a rough idea of their capabilities." Cade winked at Sara. "There's nothing they can wreck on the ranch."

"I doubt your horses will think so after they leave."

"Please, I'd love to have you bring them. Is Saturday okay?"

"You're sure?"

"Positive." Cade scooped both boys in his arms for a good-bye hug. He thanked them for drawing him the pictures and promised to hang them up at home.

To the twins' delight, Reese agreed they could visit the ranch on Saturday. Once a time was chosen, Reese hurried the kids out to his car, trying to hush their loud and prolonged goodbye calls to Cade.

"So, Sara, you're now free to discuss Mr. Porter's wedding."

Sara struggled to smile, remembering the windows.

"Would it be okay if we talked at that coffee shop around the corner?" Cade asked. "I haven't had my quota of java yet, and I wouldn't mind something to eat. I think I'll need my energy to make all these decisions you're talking about."

"It's—"

"A wonderful idea!" Katie's smile resembled that of an obsequious slave. "Take as long as you like, Sara. We want to do our best for Mr. Porter."

"Please, call me Cade."

Sara frowned at Katie. Earlier her sister had bawled her out for redoing the display mannequin's makeup instead of attending to the massive files stacked behind the reception desk. Now suddenly Katie was all smiles and pleasantness at the prospect of having Sara leave the building?

Something was fishy.

"The desk will be unattended," she reminded softly. "I could be gone a while."

"I'll find someone else." Katie's smile never wavered.

Cade cleared his throat. "If the arrangement isn't to your liking, Ms.—"

"Her name is Sara. Sara Woodward." Katie's Cheshire cat smile widened.

"It's nice to meet you, Sara," Cade said softly, his smile charming. "But I repeat, if the arrangement isn't to Sara's liking…"

Nothing about her current circumstances was to Sara's liking. Her "liking" would be to work with Gideon Glen—a special-effects genius whose work Sara had admired for years. Sara's biggest "liking" would be for her family to accept her independence and stop trying to coax her back into the family business.

But she could hardly say that in front of a client. Instead Sara leaned forward, grasped her sister's arm and excused herself.

"We'll just be a moment, Mr. Porter."

"It's Cade."

"Of course it is." Sara dragged Katie around the corner.

"Sara!" Katie struggled to free her arm. "What are you doing?"

"Consulting. Katie, this guy doesn't have the first clue about a wedding." She kept her voice subdued through rigid control.

"You'll figure it out. Work with him. And take your time," Katie said sweetly. Too sweetly.

Warning bells chimed a second time, but all Sara could do was ignore their caution and follow her sister back into Woodwards' reception area.

"Enjoy your coffee, you two." Katie made it sound like a date.

Sara ached to refuse. But with Cade Porter watching—
You're home to help, remember. So help.

"Mr. Porter, how do like your coffee?"

"Strong and black." He flashed his smile and Sara's knees softened.

Those blue irises are only colored contacts.

Her knees didn't seem to care.

"Bye." Katie waggled her fingers at them before picking up the phone.

Cade opened the big glass entry door. Sara walked through, wondering if she'd imagined the smug look on Katie's face.

"Autumn's such a refreshing season, isn't it?" Mr. Porter grinned as he clapped a hand on his Stetson so the wind couldn't take it.

"I guess."

It was obvious from his deep breaths that he'd found the store confining and enjoyed the freedom of outside. Sara struggled to match her step to his. Not an easy feat wearing the needle-thin heels Katie insisted were the only appropriate footwear for a fashion-conscious house like Woodwards'. Her best effort was a mincing half jog.

When they finally arrived at the coffee shop, Sara collapsed into a chair and brushed the mass of damp tumbling curls off her face. Her look, reflected in the pastry case mirror across the room, was so *not* the image of a pulled-together career woman out for coffee with a client.

"Makeup artist, cure thyself," she muttered, patting a napkin against her damp forehead.

"Excuse me?"

"Talking to myself. Often happens after a round with the twins." Hiding facial flaws on others was Sara's passion. Hiding her own was a losing battle, so she ignored her reflection. "Somehow those two little kids always leave me feeling like

I need time to recoup. Happy but drained. The way you looked before we left the store."

"I wasn't drained," he said.

"Right." He'd been chafing to get away. Sara wondered why.

"Because I invited you, I'm buying. What will you have?" Cade leaned one shoulder against the wall, his face all sharply defined planes and angles in the dimmer interior.

"Just coffee, thanks. Double cream."

Cade's shadowed gaze raked her face, then his swift assessment moved slowly from her untamed curls to the pearly sheen of polish Katie had painted on her toenails. He nodded once, then walked to the counter.

Sara leaned back against the banquette. Because Cade wasn't volunteering any information, she'd have to come out and ask about his sister, and risk sounding like a snoop. She hadn't come up with a way to begin when her client returned, grinning as he set a gigantic cup in front of her.

"Thank you. Is something amusing you, Mr. Porter?"

"Cade." He studied her hair, frizzy now from the outside humidity. "You don't look old enough to drink that."

Sara's molars met. Tomorrow she'd cut off her curls. Perhaps then—

"I assure you I am perfectly capable of functioning as your wedding planner. I do have the necessary credentials." Later she'd ask Katie how that certificate had gone from the trunk in her room at their parents' home to hanging on Woodwards' wall.

"I'm sure you do." He sat down across from her, stretched his long legs to one side. His eyes turned a moody shade of blue.

"Is the coffee bad?" She sipped her own.

"Coffee's fine." The granite jaw softened slightly.

Sara liked the effect. "So—?"

"I wanted to do something really special for my sister. I didn't realize planning her wedding would be so complicated."

"And now you're thinking more along the lines of elopement?" she teased.

"No way." Not a morsel of doubt crept into his low, firm tone. "I specifically chose Weddings by Woodwards because they're supposed to be the best in the business. And I want the very best."

"Woodwards is top of the heap." Sara studied him. "You need the best because—?"

"Because this wedding has to be absolutely perfect. She deserves it."

As he said the words, something in Cade Porter's demeanor changed. The intensity of his voice, the love underlying his words, the blaze of pride in his blue irises—all of it told Sara how much he loved his sister.

"Your sister is lucky to have a brother like you." For a tiny second a soft brush of yearning feathered across her heart. Then reality returned.

Cade Porter was planning this wedding without the bride! It was exactly the kind of thing her lovable family would do, the kind of overbearing, know-it-all action that Sara constantly fought against.

"Tell me what your sister would want." That didn't sound nosy. Sara held her pen above the pad and waited.

Cade leaned back against his chair and closed his eyes. His deep, assured tone compelled her attention.

"She's a perfectionist. She'd want every detail to be taken care of. So do I. I don't want any surprises on that day. I want it beautiful, elegant but not stuffy. I want the guests to enjoy themselves, to feel welcome. I particularly don't want ordinary." He opened his eyes. "I want memorable. Does that help?"

"It's a place to start. Any idea when she'll hold her wedding?"

His eyes flickered open. "For now, the date's up in the air."

Another glitch.

"When will she know?"

"Probably not until a few days before it's to be held."

Sara frowned. This was getting weirder by the moment.

"Mr. Porter, we need your sister present for at least one consultation."

"Not possible."

"But it sounds like you want to have everything planned without having a set date."

"That's exactly what I want. A church ceremony seems obvious."

"Unless the wedding comes during a busy season like Christmas when we would have to book ages ahead." Sara set her cup aside, troubled by his plan.

She was pretty sure she could do this—on her own, without help. She had the skill, the ability. It was simply a matter of applying her brain to the problem and then coming up with a solution. But was it right to do it all without the bride's involvement?

"What about a park setting? Then we wouldn't need to book ahead."

His eyes narrowed, but he didn't answer.

"Weddings in a place that holds meaning for the couple can also be charming. Is there some place special to your sister and her fiancé?"

Cade seemed not to hear her because he suddenly leaned forward, holding her gaze with his own.

"If it was you, would a church wedding be your choice?"

"No." She avoided his gaze.

"Why not?"

"I'm not the church-wedding type." Sara wasn't about to

tell him how long it had been since she'd stopped talking to God. "Listen, Mr. Porter—"

"Can we please agree that you'll call me Cade?" He was doing that charm bit again, and he hadn't moved a muscle.

"Cade," she complied, pretending a coolness she didn't feel. "*My* preferences are not the issue here. I must talk to the bride to get her feelings on things."

"She's leaving it all to me."

His fast response ramped up Sara's inner warning system to red alert. She looked him straight in the eye, just the way Winnie had taught her.

"Does your sister even know you're planning this wedding?"

"Not yet." Cade's smile dimmed. "It's a surprise."

Sara squeezed her eyes closed, barely stifling her groan.

"I'm guessing you don't think that's a good idea?"

"I think it's a terrible idea. I have never known a bride who didn't want to play an active part in her own wedding." Sara glanced away, counted to five. When she looked back, his eyes waited for her. Their gazes locked. "Tell me the truth."

"She wants to elope," he rasped, his voice drained of its rich timbre. "To go somewhere no one knows her and take the most important step of her life."

"Then surely—"

"She's so fixated on getting married she can't see how much she'll regret her decision later. But I know exactly how much she might need those memories in the future." His ominous tone told Sara Cade's own personal reasons were figuring into his decision to organize this wedding.

She recognized that he was probably smarting from his sister's decision. Maybe he felt left out. Maybe he'd been goaded into circumventing what she wanted by their parents.

Whatever his reason, Sara was the last person to help Cade Porter plan something his sister didn't want. She had too much experience with interfering families and the pain that came from resisting their strong wills.

"I'm sorry, Mr. Porter. I can't help you with this wedding." Sara rose, picked up her purse. "If you still want Weddings by Woodwards, I'll select another planner. But my advice is to talk to your sister, really listen to what she tells you. Then abide by her decision."

"But—"

Sara ignored his frown, determined to make him understand.

"You want your sister to treasure happy memories of her wedding day?"

"Of course!"

"That won't happen if every anniversary she's reminded that you forced something she didn't want. She's entitled to have her own dream—even if it isn't your dream."

He couldn't know she was speaking from experience.

"But—"

"I'm sorry, I can't help you. Goodbye."

For a fraction of a second, one thought held Sara immobile. She was going to disappoint the family.

Again.

Chapter Two

"Wait!"

Cade ignored the curious stares of the other coffee-shop patrons. He needed Sara Woodward. He needed Weddings by Woodwards, needed their expertise and their clout. But more than that, he found himself not wanting this small delicate woman to think badly of him.

And she did.

Her prickly tone, the frost edging her voice, the sharp snap of her consonants—Sara Woodward had pegged him as an overbearing ogre, forcing his sister to bend to his demands.

"You don't understand."

"No, I don't."

"Will you please hear me out before judging me any further?"

Sara debated for a moment, nodded once then took her seat.

Cade smiled.

"Thank you. I can imagine what you think, Sara. But if I couldn't, your face gives it away." Relieved she was still listening, he hurried on. "I apologize. I should have started at the beginning. I've lived alone so long, I expect people to read my mind."

"You don't have to apologize. I still won't do it." The jut of her chin emphasized her determination.

"Give me five minutes?"

She studied him, lips pursed. Finally she nodded.

"I'll listen. But it's really a moot point."

"Why?"

"Unless the wedding takes place very quickly, I won't be around. I'd have to hand you over to someone else eventually anyway."

Someone else? But he'd connected with her. Or thought he had.

"I understood that once Weddings by Woodwards took on an event, their planner stayed until the event was over."

"Usually that's true." Her lids drooped, shielding her eyes.

"So?" What was she hiding? Cade leaned in to study her closed-up face.

"I won't be staying. I returned to Woodwards to help out only while my grandmother is ill."

"Returned from?"

"Los Angeles." Sara studied her notepad. "We can go back to the store now. Katie will help you."

"She said she's booked today." Cade dismissed that. "You don't know when you're leaving Denver?"

"Not exactly." Sara avoided his gaze. "But the moment Winnie is back at Woodwards full-time, I'm off to L.A. Working at Weddings by Woodwards is temporary for me."

Her voice, sheathed in steely determination, gave the impression it wasn't the first time she'd said that. Cade didn't argue. Instead he signaled to their server to refill their cups and offered her one of the croissants he'd ordered.

"You said you'd explain," Sara prodded.

"I'm not sure where to start." Cade stirred his coffee, then decided it wasn't going to get easier. "Karen, my sister, is overseas, in the military."

"Oh?"

"She and her fiancé are in a special tactical force. I hear from her sporadically. In her last e-mail Karen told me she and Trent had just become engaged and that they wanted to be married as soon as they return, at the end of their mission, which is secret. See why I can't specify a date and time?"

"Yes, I understand." Interest lit her expressive face.

"Karen's twenty-three," he continued. "She and Trent were high-school sweethearts. I want to give her the kind of wedding our parents would have. A celebration."

"But *she* wants to elope."

"Because Karen thinks it will be easier on me, that it won't cost me anything, won't make a fuss I'll have to endure." Publicizing personal details wasn't his forte, but Cade could tell by Sara's dubious expression that he was going to have to open up if he wanted her help. "You see, I was supposed to be married right before Karen went overseas the first time. My fiancée died two weeks before the wedding."

He heard her soft gasp.

"I'm so sorry."

"Thanks." Cade hated this part, wanted to get past it fast. "Marnie died of an aneurysm. It was totally unexpected."

"And then your sister left." Her face softened. "That was a hard time for you."

"Yes." He could see Sara didn't understand. Yet. He'd have to give her more details. "Karen felt guilty for leaving right after I'd lost Marnie. She wanted to ask the Army for leave, but I persuaded her to go."

"Because?" Sara's brown velvet eyes missed nothing.

"Because she deserves to build her own life. There was

nothing she could do for me. I'm older, I'm stronger. I could get through it on my own."

"You wanted to protect her."

Cade smiled at the accuracy of her assessment and the skill with which she cut through his prevarication.

"It's what I do," he admitted.

"You protect your sister—because you think Karen isn't capable of looking after herself?" Disbelief emphasized the arch of one sculpted eyebrow. "At twenty-three?"

"You remind me of her." Cade recalled the many times his sister had cut through his excuses and demanded the truth. "Karen doesn't mince words, either."

The petite blond wedding planner tightened her lips.

"It doesn't have anything to do with how old she is, Sara." Cade let the story pour out. "Our parents died when I was eighteen. Karen was ten. I raised her. I was her father, mother and her brother. She's my only family. That's why this wedding has to be special."

"Even if she doesn't want it?" Sara's brows furrowed.

"She does! She just doesn't want to let on she does because Karen thinks another wedding will bring back the pain of losing Marnie."

"Will it?"

"Probably some," he acknowledged. "But my experiencing a little pain isn't a good enough reason not to have a wedding for Karen."

"I see."

She didn't.

"My sister used to constantly talk about what she'd do for her own wedding. She had more bride dolls than any of her friends. In her room at home there's a big fat album full of wedding pictures she's been cutting out of magazines for as long as I can remember." Cade met her stare. "Karen's wedding has been a dream she's had forever. I am not going to let her give it up because of me."

"Generous of you. The album might come in handy." Sara's wise-owl eyes never left his face. "But surely you understand what's involved? You were about to be married. You must have consulted with your fiancée, made joint decisions."

That made him laugh.

"If you'd known Marnie, you wouldn't have said that. She was the ultimate organizer and she did not like her plans interfered with. That was fine by me. Some stuff was going on at the ranch at the time and I was glad to let her handle all the details. I didn't care how, as long as we got married." He made a face. "I wish now I'd paid more attention."

"You've known a lot of loss."

"I've known a lot of happiness," he corrected. "I thank God for that every day."

Sara's face closed up like a clam, her eyes dropped to her worksheet. Cade wondered what he'd said wrong.

"It isn't possible to ask Karen's preferences on anything?"

Cade shook his head.

"She and Trent were leaving base for a new mission the day she e-mailed me. I can leave messages, but I can't contact her directly. Even if I could, there wouldn't be any point."

"Because?"

"Because all Karen and Trent care about is getting married as soon as they get home. That's why I want everything in place." He wouldn't give up, not yet. "I don't want my sister to elope because it's easier. I want her to come home, to walk her down the aisle of the church we grew up in. I want to hand her care over to her husband."

Not strictly accurate, but Cade pushed past the half truth to continue.

"I want her to have precious memories of her wedding day that she can take out and treasure when the tough patches come."

At last Sara lifted her head and met his gaze.

"It's going to be a lot of work."

Cade's heart bumped with relief. That meant she was going to help, didn't it?

"Life is a lot of work. But family matters, and when you do something for them, the payoff on their faces makes the work seem like play." He studied her. "You must know that yourself."

"I must, mustn't I?" Sara agreed dourly, her concentration on the scribbles she placed on her notepad.

The chagrin tingeing her voice surprised Cade. He studied her profile, followed one of her golden ringlets to its resting place on her narrow shoulder. Sara Woodward had the kind of soft, wistful beautiful many women tried to erase.

Perhaps she—

A movement outside caught Cade's attention and he blinked at the man who peered through the glass.

"Isn't that your brother, Reese, father of the infamous twins?"

Sara's head jerked up. She twisted to get a better look. When she turned back, her almost-black eyes glittered with indignation.

"Yes, it's Reese." Sara squished her napkin into a ball. "Sometimes I wish I'd never left L.A."

Her whisper shocked Cade. Fairly certain she hadn't been talking to him, he didn't press because her face looked as if she'd lost her best friend.

Sara's narrow shoulders drooped. The soft cre~~ ~~ blouse shifted, revealing her slim neck and the ~~d~~ scarf she'd tucked in there. Cade didn't kno~~w~~ fashion, but he was fairly certain that par~~t~~

ribbean orange wasn't in vogue at the moment. Yet on Sara it looked exactly right—vibrant, warm, full of potential.

He wondered why she'd chosen the shade. Actually he had a thousand questions about his wedding planner.

"What do you do when you're in L.A., Sara?"

She blinked. Big innocent doe eyes, an unusual combination with that blond hair, widened.

"Do?" Her cheekbones turned a richer pink. "Um…"

"You don't have to tell me if you don't want to." He'd only just met the woman and now he was prying? Loneliness wasn't an excuse. "I'm getting too personal. Sorry."

"It's not a secret. I'm a makeup artist for a movie studio. I'm trying to break into special effects, though." She said it defiantly, as if she expected him to offer some negative remark on her choice of career.

"Cool." Cade asked the first thing he thought of. "Ever worked with the stars?"

"Once or twice." Her eyelids drooped, shielding her thoughts. One short oval nail tapped against the tabletop.

Sara might not like his questions, but at least she hadn't told him to mind his own business. Cade pressed on.

"I'm guessing it's a challenging field."

"It can be." She lifted her chin and her face transformed, skin glowing, eyes shining with excitement. "That's what I like about it. It's a chance to prove you can change things, make them into what you want. I never tire of that."

The hint of defiance underlying her words reminded him of Karen on the day she'd announced she'd enlisted. Determination. Grit. Challenge.

Sara's fingertips tightened around her cup of barely touched coffee.

"I'm going to get into special effects. As soon as I can figure out how."

one sister and one brother that he knew of, and a grandmother who could be called upon if needed. Everything he longed for.

So why did she seem so desperate to run away from them?

"Families are precious. They should be treasured," he said, and wished he hadn't when she tossed a glare toward the window and her brother.

"I do treasure my family. Very much." Her jaw thrust out an inch farther. "But sometimes I have to escape them."

"Why?"

"Let's get back to your wedding." Sara ignored the question, tapped her notepad. "Are we settled on a church for the ceremony?"

Cade kept his focus on her, wishing she'd explain.

"Or you could wait till my grandmother is back."

"I don't want to wait." It took about ten seconds to reach a decision. Cade sat up straight, pushed his shoulders back. "I'll think about a location. In the meantime, what else do I need to decide to get this thing rolling?"

"Without a firm date it's difficult to plan a lot, but you could begin to consider invitations, color schemes." Sara raised one eyebrow. "I'm guessing you won't choose the bride's dress?"

"Given your current job, I guess that question is understandable." He grinned, leaned back in his seat, senses enmeshed in the spicy fragrance of her perfume. "Think more 'big picture,' Sara."

"What? Most brides think clothes are a very important part of wedding. Wedding gowns, tuxedos." She chuckled at his huff of distaste and continued.

But the more she listed, the more Cade felt like a man drowning. Sara must have noticed because she finally paused.

"It's a lot to handle," she said, her voice softening. "Maybe you need to rethink this idea."

"I'm sure you will." He remembered an earlier comment. "It was nice of you to put your dream on hold to help out while your grandmother recuperates."

"I didn't want to." Soft pink deepened to a rose blush.

"But you came anyway. That's true commitment." Cade studied the pure clear shape of her face. "Surely there must be a call for your kind of work in Denver?"

"For makeup. But I'm trying to get into special effects. That means Hollywood."

"I see."

"Do you?" Sara Woodward's velvet brown eyes challenged him to understand.

And Cade didn't, though he wished he could.

For him, family came right behind his love for God. Although his parents had been gone for fifteen years, he still treasured the family moments he could recall, happy, laughing moments when it seemed as if they'd always be there, providing the love and security he'd taken for granted.

The same love he'd showered on Karen as he tried to protect her.

He'd compared them, but Cade now realized Sara Woodward was nothing like his sister. Karen was a product of her environment, strong and tough like the land abutting the Rockies. Sara, with her dainty figure, exotic scarf and that mass of bouncing golden curls, was more like one of Karen's delicate porcelain wedding dolls, the ones that belonged in a glass box on a high shelf where the hard knocks of life could not reach.

And yet, in the depths of Sara's eyes he caught a glimpse of a woman with inner fire and determination. But she was not comfortable with her world.

Cade couldn't make the pieces fit. Sara had family here, guaranteed job security in the family business. She had at least

ribbean orange wasn't in vogue at the moment. Yet on Sara
it looked exactly right—vibrant, warm, full of potential.

He wondered why she'd chosen the shade. Actually he had
a thousand questions about his wedding planner.

"What do you do when you're in L.A., Sara?"

She blinked. Big innocent doe eyes, an unusual combination with that blond hair, widened.

"Do?" Her cheekbones turned a richer pink. "Um…"

"You don't have to tell me if you don't want to." He'd only
just met the woman and now he was prying? Loneliness
wasn't an excuse. "I'm getting too personal. Sorry."

"It's not a secret. I'm a makeup artist for a movie studio.
I'm trying to break into special effects, though." She said it
defiantly, as if she expected him to offer some negative remark on her choice of career.

"Cool." Cade asked the first thing he thought of. "Ever
worked with the stars?"

"Once or twice." Her eyelids drooped, shielding her
thoughts. One short oval nail tapped against the tabletop.

Sara might not like his questions, but at least she hadn't
told him to mind his own business. Cade pressed on.

"I'm guessing it's a challenging field."

"It can be." She lifted her chin and her face transformed,
skin glowing, eyes shining with excitement. "That's what I
like about it. It's a chance to prove you can change things,
make them into what you want. I never tire of that."

The hint of defiance underlying her words reminded him
of Karen on the day she'd announced she'd enlisted. Determination. Grit. Challenge.

Sara's fingertips tightened around her cup of barely
touched coffee.

"I'm going to get into special effects. As soon as I can figure out how."

"I want her to have precious memories of her wedding day that she can take out and treasure when the tough patches come."

At last Sara lifted her head and met his gaze.

"It's going to be a lot of work."

Cade's heart bumped with relief. That meant she was going to help, didn't it?

"Life is a lot of work. But family matters, and when you do something for them, the payoff on their faces makes the work seem like play." He studied her. "You must know that yourself."

"I must, mustn't I?" Sara agreed dourly, her concentration on the scribbles she placed on her notepad.

The chagrin tingeing her voice surprised Cade. He studied her profile, followed one of her golden ringlets to its resting place on her narrow shoulder. Sara Woodward had the kind of soft, wistful beautiful many women tried to erase.

Perhaps she—

A movement outside caught Cade's attention and he blinked at the man who peered through the glass.

"Isn't that your brother, Reese, father of the infamous twins?"

Sara's head jerked up. She twisted to get a better look. When she turned back, her almost-black eyes glittered with indignation.

"Yes, it's Reese." Sara squished her napkin into a ball. "Sometimes I wish I'd never left L.A."

Her whisper shocked Cade. Fairly certain she hadn't been talking to him, he didn't press because her face looked as if she'd lost her best friend.

Sara's narrow shoulders drooped. The soft cream silk blouse shifted, revealing her slim neck and the delicate silk scarf she'd tucked in there. Cade didn't know much about fashion, but he was fairly certain that particular hue of Ca-

Maybe he did. Nothing about organizing Karen's wedding seemed as simple as it had back on the ranch. But that didn't mean Cade was giving up.

"I need a little time to wrap my mind around the details, that's all."

"Take all the time you need. I better get back to work."

While Sara dabbed her lips on a napkin, Cade tossed some money on the table, then led the way outside, holding her arm until she pulled it away.

He checked the sidewalk, expecting to see Reese.

"I guess your brother had to leave."

"Yeah. Probably to give his report."

"Report?" He didn't understand that comment, or what had drained the sparkle from her eyes, but the Woodward family wasn't his business. "Because Reese isn't here, I'll walk you back to the store."

"Thanks, but I can manage without you or my brother to guide me. I've been finding my own way around L.A. for a while now." Hostility leeched through the sour words.

"I don't doubt you can." Cade hadn't sensed tension between sister and brother earlier, which made him even more curious about the Woodwards, especially about Sara. "I have to walk there anyway. My car's parked across from the store."

"Oh. Right. Sorry." She walked beside him in a mincing pace, almost falling flat on her face when her heel caught in a sidewalk crack. She recovered quickly, tossed him a smile. "I thought all cowboys drove trucks?"

"I don't bring my truck into town unless I'm hauling something. Too many bad drivers ready to dent it. And, yes, all the stories about ranchers treating their trucks like babies are true. Hey!" Cade grabbed her just in time and held on until Sara had regained her balance again. "Are those things comfortable?"

"Not in the least," Sara told him, fingers pressing into his arm as she righted herself. "But Katie insists they're the only appropriate footwear for my work at Woodwards. I usually work in sneakers and jeans."

"I imagine you look very nice in those, too." A sense of loss suffused him when her arm slid out from his. "Oh, we're here already."

"Whenever you want to talk again, stop in." Sara's eyes lost their brooding, lightened to a rich cocoa. "We'll do our best to help. But I think you should wait and talk to Karen. Then listen. She might have other reasons for wanting to elope."

"Like what?" Cade resented the inference that he didn't know exactly how Karen thought. His baby sister was an open book to him.

"Talk to her. She'll tell you."

"Will you be here if I come back?"

"I don't know." An internal struggle turned her eyes a shade of bittersweet. "Probably."

The expressionless gaze she'd first assumed at the store, the "mask" look that hid her emotions, slid into place. He disliked it intensely.

"Well, thanks for coffee and the croissants." Sara's clear natural glow reminded Cade of the foothills of his ranch where mountain springs tumbled down in a rush of sparkling droplets chased by sunbeams. Her orange scarf was like a mountain lily.

Cade blinked. Loneliness was definitely affecting him.

"You've given me a lot of wedding details to think about. What if we meet tomorrow?"

Sara's eyes widened with surprise.

"You mean, you still want me to work with you, even though I'm not staying?"

"You have an original perspective. Karen would like that."

His sister's penchant for the uncommon had often been a source of contention between them.

"You must miss her a lot."

Cade hadn't realized how much until he met Sara.

"Karen hasn't lived at home full-time for ages, but when she did, life was good. With my sister around there was always something going on. She enriched my life, made it fun. I miss that. I miss her."

Sara went very still. Her face tilted upward as she studied him. Cade stood immobile under her scrutiny, waiting for the question he saw reflected in her eyes. But she didn't ask.

So suddenly it made him catch his breath, her face altered, her voice emerged warm and generous.

"I'm just the substitute at Woodwards, so I don't have any regular clients, which means I have a lot of free time. I could meet you whenever you like to brainstorm something wonderful for Karen's wedding."

Cade wasn't about to waste his opportunity.

"I have to be in town tomorrow morning for some business. Could you meet me at Cartier's Café at noon?"

"Cartier's? Sure. But Woodwards has lots of—" Sara blinked, then waggled a finger at him, eyes twinkling. "You're trying to avoid going back into the store, aren't you?"

"If at all possible," he admitted honestly. "How did you guess?"

"Your face. Lots of men find the environment a little— overpowering. The family has been trying to get Winnie to scale back, at least in reception."

"But?"

Sara shrugged.

"Granny Winnie is an incurable romantic, that's how she got started in this business. Yards of tulle, tons of hearts and flowers—it's been a part of her world for so long I doubt she could envision Woodwards any other way now."

"Why should she?" Cade tilted his head back to study the ivory stone facade of the building. "Her way obviously works. I was told Weddings by Woodwards assisted with more than four hundred weddings last year."

"And each of them was absolutely perfect. That's my family." There it was again, that proud but irritated tone. "How did you choose Woodwards, Cade?"

"I talked to some friends of Karen who told me that if I wanted a spectacular wedding, Weddings by Woodwards was the only way."

"I see." Sara's eyes narrowed. She made a notation on her pad, then lifted her head, brown eyes narrowed. "These friends—are they good friends? The kind of friends your sister would ask to be her attendants if she were planning her own wedding?"

Cade slowly nodded. Sara Woodward may have been out of the family business for a while, but she caught on to his line of thinking faster than the ranch foreman who'd been working for him for ten years.

"Exactly that kind of friend," he told her.

She grinned, her eyes dancing.

"Now we're cooking. Tonight I want you to write down everything you can think of about Karen. Bring your notes and her album tomorrow. That will give us a place to start."

"Okay."

Sara was easy to talk to. Cade surprised himself by prattling on and on about how much he wanted his sister to come home, how he worried about her safety, fussed about her future happiness.

When Sara's attention slipped from him, Cade turned, saw a diminutive figure in black in the display window, writing in big brown letters.

Do you want your wedding to look like this?

"That's Winnie!"

"But I thought—" Cade trailed behind Sara into the store, right up to the narrow door from which she'd first emerged. He halted, knowing how tight the fit was.

Sara slipped through.

"Winnie? What are you doing here?"

He heard a forced cough, then a familiar voice that didn't sound the least bit ill.

"Hello, darling. I thought I'd stop by to check on things. I figured the twins must have rearranged the window, so I—"

"Never mind the twins," Sara scolded. "You're supposed to be at home. Resting. Come on, out you go."

Cade stepped back as Sara emerged, leading her grandmother. He'd only seen photographs of Winifred Woodward, but she looked exactly like the elegant duchess in her publicity photos. Today she wore a black sheath dress with silver jewelry and high heels. She looked significantly younger than her rumored age. Her silver white curls were swept up into a regal style that enhanced merry brown eyes and rose-tinted cheekbones.

"You're Cade Porter, I think." She thrust out a tiny blue-veined hand to grasp his. "Winifred Woodward. I'm so sorry I couldn't keep our appointment."

"I'm sorry you're not well." Except she looked the picture of health.

"It's just a cold. My family is overreacting." Winnie patted Sara's cheek. "I'm getting better every day."

"You don't sound better. Your voice is scratchy." Sara frowned. "How did you get here, Grandmother?"

"A cab." She brushed her fingers against Sara's golden curls. "Don't be angry, dear. I couldn't sit around that house a moment longer. I'm used to being busy."

"Katie said the doctors ordered rest. You're to follow their advice, Granny. That's why I came." She grasped the old lady's arm as Winifred tried to stem a bout of coughing. "Now you've tired yourself out. Home you go."

"I never thought you'd try to tell me what to do." Winifred's perfectly made-up face wore a sly look. "You, of all people, Sara. Aren't you the one who's always championing your right to live your life your own way?"

"I'm not sick. And my doctor didn't tell me to stay in bed."

"I thought I heard—Grandmother?" Katie rushed into the room and, seizing the older woman's arm, seated her in one of the fussy chairs that littered the foyer. "Look at you. Your face is as white as a calla lily. You'll probably faint any moment."

Cade thought Katie's concern was exaggerated considering Winifred hadn't exhibited any sign of fainting. But it was nice to see the old lady was cherished.

"I'm fine," Winifred repeated. Her smile looked slightly forced now.

"You're not. Your hand is too warm and you're sniffling."

"She's going home, Katie. I'll take her." Sara shuffled papers on the desktop, obviously searching for something. "Do you know where my car keys are? I'm sure I left them beside the phone."

"Oh, dear."

Katie fluttered her eyelashes at him, then pressed her fingertips against her lips. In Cade's opinion this was the sister who belonged in Hollywood, except Katie's acting was too forced. And why was she looking at him like that?

"Is something wrong?"

"Well, you see, Reese's car wouldn't start," Katie said. "He had to get to another appointment, so I gave him Sara's car keys. I didn't think she'd need them and he promised he wouldn't be long."

"Then I'll take yours, Katie." Sara held out her hand.

"No! You can't have them." Katie's shrill voice broke on a nervous laugh at their stares of surprise. "I mean, that's the problem. I put my car in the shop this morning for an oil change. If I'd known we'd need it—"

Something about Katie's quick response bothered him, but Cade wasn't going to speculate. He needed to get back to the ranch. But when Mrs. Woodward's thin form shuddered and another cough rattled her tiny figure, he put his own plans aside.

"I'll be happy to drive you home, ma'am. My car's just across the street."

"Don't be silly. I'll call a cab." She wheezed out the words, her handkerchief muffling something he didn't quite catch.

"It's not a problem. Please, allow me." Cade held out his arm, surprised by the weakness of her grip when she rose. The old lady must be sicker than she looked. "I could bring the car around to the front door if it's too difficult for you to walk."

"I'm fine. Sara, where's my coat? Oh, good. Now you come here on the other side where I can hold on to you. All of a sudden I've gone a bit wobbly."

Sara obeyed immediately, casting him an apologetic look behind her grandmother's back.

Cade told himself to mind his own business when it seemed Winifred fussed needlessly. To her credit, Sara kept softly reassuring her as they crossed the street to his car. Winifred insisted on sitting in the back. Alone.

"I can spread out then," she husked, her voice significantly worse than it had been moments earlier. She closed her eyes. "I'll rest a few moments. I'm a bit tired. I gave Vivian the day off, so I'll need Sara to help me to bed. Perhaps you wouldn't mind waiting to drive her back here, Cade. It would be so kind of you."

"No." Sara glanced at him. "It's not necessary, Grandmother."

"No worries." Cade held open her door, waited until Sara was seated. As he closed the door, he noted Winifred's sparkling eyes and the funny smile lifting her lips. When she saw him watching, she quickly shut her eyes.

He got in the driver's seat, curiosity rampant.

"If you turn right at the next corner, we'll go that way. Winnie lives in Cherry Creek." Sara glanced over one shoulder as if she worried about disturbing her grandmother.

Cherry Creek was the "old money" side of town, filled with posh houses and beautiful landscapes. Cade drove toward it silently, content to watch the exchanges between the two.

Her affectionate care of her grandmother was admirable, but Cade didn't think this was the real Sara. She was hiding her true feelings. Personally, he far preferred the honest, open woman with whom he'd shared croissants at the coffee shop to this dutiful person who slavishly agreed with every demand her grandmother made. But he kept silent as Sara handed the old woman out of the car and ushered her into the house.

"It's nice of you to offer, but I'll stay here," she said five minutes later when she returned. They were alone and the real Sara was back.

"You want me to disobey her edict that I drive you back to the store?"

"Yes. I want to make sure Granny goes right to bed."

"Okay. What time is good for tomorrow?" He saw she'd forgotten.

"Tomor— Oh, lunch." Sara frowned. "When I agreed to help out in the store, I told Katie I'd take a noon lunch hour. Does that work for you?" She tried to step backward and lost her balance.

"Perfect." Cade steadied her with a grin. "But in case you change shoes between now and then, I better make sure I know exactly who I'm meeting. How tall are you—without the stilts?" He enjoyed the flush of color dotting her cheekbones.

"Never mind," was all she said, making it obvious she had height issues.

"Ah. What other secrets are you hiding? A glass eye? Wooden leg?"

Sara lifted one eyebrow. "I'll never tell."

"That's an invitation I can't resist." Cade pulled open his car door. "Tomorrow, twelve noon at Cartier's. Bring your ideas."

"I should probably warn you, some of my ideas have been called a little, um, off the wall." Sara tilted her head to one side, studying his reaction.

A wayward ringlet danced in the breeze, then settled against her cheek in a gentle caress. Cade swallowed.

"It's the off-the-wall ideas that usually turn out best, Sara Woodward," he said softly so the old woman leaning out the window above them wouldn't hear. "Don't you know that yet?"

"I know. I wasn't sure you did." She grinned. "Cade Porter, this might be fun."

He got into the car, his knees as weak as if he just climbed off his horse after a four-day trail ride. "I believe it will be."

He drove back to the ranch slowly, savoring the memory of Sara's smile, a picture that stuck with him long after he should have been immersed in the mundane duties of his day.

But later that night, staring up at the stars, Cade knew daydreaming about a woman like Sara Woodward was pointless. He'd lost his chance for love and family the day Marnie died. That's when he'd known that God's will for him didn't include his cherished dream of a wife and family of his own.

So Cade would ignore his emotional draw to Sara Wood-

ward. He'd concentrate on throwing Karen the best wedding
he could. He'd continue to hope and pray his sister would
choose to live at the ranch or at least nearby. Most of all, he'd
accept that his future was to be a solitary one. He had to. He'd
learned his lesson too well.

When God made up His mind, He didn't change it.

Chapter Three

"You're spending a lot of time in front of the mirror this morning, sis. Any special reason?"

"If you had to cart those musty old wedding catalogs out of the storeroom, you'd be checking yourself for dust, too." Sara avoided Katie's quizzical gaze. "I'm not sure why you chose me for that crummy job, but I sure got filthy. I'm glad you forgot you'd left this suit from the cleaners here. I needed a change."

"You look great in it."

"Thanks. I worked up an appetite, too. I can hardly wait for lunch."

"Hmm." Katie turned away, checked the clock. "It's early, but you might as well go now, while it's quiet. Who knows what the afternoon will bring?"

"As long as it's not more dust." She paused, chose her words carefully. "I'm meeting someone for lunch, so I probably won't be back early."

Sara had expected her sister to start asking questions. Yet Katie seemed oddly uninterested in anything except the computer in front of her.

"Fine."

"Okay, then, see you later."

"Uh-huh." Katie didn't even glance at her. That was odd.

Sara stepped through the door and lifted her face, reveling in the sun's warmth. Even L.A. weather couldn't match the startling clarity of an October morning in Denver. Crisp leaves hung in shimmering burned umber against the cerulean sky. Tiny gusts of wind danced several fallen ones across the sidewalk in front of her. They crackled when she stepped on them.

God's in His heaven, all's right with the world.

Adam Woodward, Sara's grandfather, had penned Robert Browning's famous poem in his diary many times in the last months of his life. In her senior year of high school, when Sara had discovered the leather-bound volume, she'd read it. There she'd felt more kinship with a man she'd never met than she'd ever known with her family.

She'd begged Winnie to provide other journals and poured over them, too, identifying with her grandfather's yearning to leave Europe and the family pottery business to make his own mark in America. The porcelain doll faces Winnie kept in a special glass case proved Grandpa Adam's talent. They also whetted Sara's creative itch.

Her grandfather's faith was the one thing Sara couldn't share. She'd never felt the close bond with God that her grandfather wrote about, never felt accepted or approved of by God. Never felt she fit into the image the minister described. Her family's easy faith made Sara uncomfortable in church, as if she didn't measure up. As if she didn't have the right to be there, to pretend she belonged where she so clearly didn't.

Years later not a lot had changed in her faith journey.

Sara quashed an inner voice that asked her why and instead concentrated on the beautiful day.

The nonlethal shoes Sara borrowed from Abby Franklin,

Woodwards' chief jeweler, made the two-block walk to Cartier's fly past. Sara wouldn't admit her light heart had a thing to do with the fact that she would see Cade Porter in a few minutes. Of course not. He was a client, a very nice one, but only a client. But she couldn't dislodge a tiny tremor of anticipation quaking in her midsection.

Until reality hit.

"Mother?" Sara flopped against the entrance column in a rush of disbelief. Her parents were in Italy. That was why she'd had to come home to help out.

"Hello, darling!" Fiona Woodward enveloped Sara in a cloud of expensive perfume. "It's wonderful to see you again." After a moment she drew away. "Love that suit."

"Thanks." Sara knew from experience how easily her mother could evade questions. "What are you doing here, Mom? I thought you were—"

"In Italy. We were." Fiona preened a little, flashing an anniversary ring Sara had never seen before. "Your father and I flew home this morning, a few days early so we could help with the big society wedding on Saturday. We decided to stop for lunch before going to the store. Are you home for a while?"

A quick scan of the restaurant showed Sara that Cade had not yet arrived. Given her mother's insatiable curiosity about every detail of her life, Sara considered that a definite blessing.

"Honey?" Her mother twisted to survey the area. "Are you meeting someone?"

There was no point prevaricating. Her mother would find out. She always did. Then the questions would be nonstop.

"I am meeting a friend for lunch." Sara opened her eyes wide and smiled innocently. "But I want to hear all about your trip."

"Meaning you'll be in town for a few days?" Her mother's eyes sparkled. "How lovely. We'll have time to talk. I must run now, though. Your father went to snag a cab."

Grandma Winnie!

"Mom, there's something you should—"

"No time now, darling. Later. After work." With a quick buss cheek to cheek, Fiona rushed away, high heels tapping against the concrete.

Sara raised her hand to call her back, but her mother closed the door on a cab and it was too late to say anything to prepare them for Winnie's illness. Well, maybe it was better if Katie did it. They'd listen to her.

Good thing Cade wasn't here yet. No telling how long her mother would have stayed if she'd known about him. Why hadn't she refused to help him? Getting involved in his sister's wedding would only give the family more leverage. Now her parents were back, maybe she could return to L.A., although she'd go without having done any of the special-effects work she'd hoped to begin.

A hand brushed her arm.

"Hello." Cade's blue eyes sparkled in the sunshine. "Been waiting long?"

"Actually I just arrived."

"Bad morning?" His hand rested against her waist as he escorted her to the maître d's desk.

Sara pretended nonchalance while her heart leaped at the contact.

"My mother was here."

"I'm sorry I missed her."

I'm not.

"She and my father have been in Italy, celebrating their anniversary. I had no idea they were coming back today. I don't think anyone else does, either." In fact, judging by Katie's plan to clear out storerooms, Sara was certain her parents were supposed to be gone for at least another week.

Fiona mentioned a big society wedding, but no one had

told Sara. She ignored the tiny twinge of hurt she felt at being left out. How silly to feel hurt. She wasn't a *real* employee at Woodwards. She didn't want to be.

"Your parents came home because of your grandmother?"

"I don't think they know about her yet. I thought the family was keeping it a secret so my parents could enjoy their well-deserved vacation."

"Maybe someone decided it was better if they knew the truth."

"I guess." But no one had told her that, either, which bugged Sara.

They were seated at a window table overlooking Cartier's delightful garden. Outside, golden sheaves of mature grasses waved in the breeze. A few flowers, unscathed from last night's frost, still bloomed.

"I haven't been here before. Thanks for asking me." Sara accepted from the waiter the heavy white card with the day's menu on it. "I'll look, but after those buttery croissants yesterday, I'm on salad for a while."

"Aw, come on. You can't expect me to enjoy my meal while you're nibbling rabbit food." Cade's white teeth flashed.

"I guess soup would be okay." With those blue eyes staring, Sara wasn't sure she'd be able to swallow a thing.

"The kind of soup should make a difference." Cade grinned.

"Why?" She couldn't quite interpret his smug tone.

"I was told mushroom is your favorite." He lifted the card from her hands and handed it, with his own, to the waiter. Then he ordered for both of them. "I think you'll enjoy this meal, Sara."

"Will I?"

The waiter brought their soup and set it down while she fumed. Cade Porter was a human bulldozer. Just like her family. Sara itched to point out his peremptory attitude, but that wasn't the way one treated a client.

Cade must have caught on.

"That wasn't very bright of me. I'm sorry, Sara. Karen would bawl me out for ordering for her without even asking. I apologize. Should I call the waiter back?"

"Never mind."

"Thank you. Shall I say grace?"

She nodded, waited until he'd finished. The word *charming* had obviously been created to describe Cade Porter. He waited for her to pick up her spoon.

That's when his words sank in.

"Who told you mushroom soup is my favorite?"

"Your sister."

"Katie." Sara closed her eyes as she smothered a groan. "When?"

"I phoned you this morning to confirm. You were out, so I spoke to her. I wanted to make sure you wouldn't have a problem with the food here. She clarified things." He frowned at her inelegant sniff.

"Oh, I'm sure she did," Sara grated. No wonder her sister had given her the dirtiest job in the building, "found" a fresh outfit and almost pushed her out the door. "What else did Katie tell you?"

"Does it matter? Why don't you taste the soup?"

She'd lost her appetite, but that wasn't his fault. Cade couldn't know, would have no idea of the lengths her family would go to keep her at Woodwards. But Katie's questions about Cade now made sense. Her sister had manipulated her hoping she'd get busy with Cade's wedding and stick around.

"I'll send it back."

"No, please. It's fine." Sara swallowed her frustration, picked up her spoon and tasted the soup. "Delicious."

"I know. This place has the best food you'll find in town." Cade made no attempt to smother his satisfaction. "You can't deny that."

"No, I can't. I apologize for my bad humor." His steady scrutiny made her nervous, so she concentrated on eating.

Silence stretched long and tense. Finally Cade pressed back in his chair and sighed.

"You would have preferred if I hadn't spoken about you to Katie." His frown turned into a quizzical ruffle. "I get that, okay?"

"Great." Her spirit groaned. Her parents were back in town. By now Katie had probably told them all about this meeting and they were all hatching another scheme.

"I promise I won't do it again."

"Thanks. I appreciate your discretion."

"I can be very discreet," Cade assured her. But his eyes wouldn't release hers and a frown now marred the smooth perfection of his forehead. "Only—"

"Yes?"

"Is there something you're not telling me?"

She had to explain. Otherwise he'd get tricked into their manipulations and maybe expect more—Sara shoved a mass of unruly ringlets behind her ear and dived in.

"Cade, I understand that you love your sister."

"As, I'm sure, you love your family." He said it casually, with the assurance of someone completely confident in his family's love.

"I do love them. Very much. But—" she waited until the salads were served and they were alone again "—my family is a pain."

It sounded horrible, but it was the truth.

Cade laughed.

"All families are at some time or another, I suppose." A

small smile played around his firm lips. "It's the nature of the beast."

Sara's stomach clenched. She looked through the window, bending her head so the ringlets swung forward, offering him no opportunity to read her expression.

"It's a little more than that in my case," she said quietly. "My family believes my move to Los Angeles to pursue my career is a terrible mistake. They've tried, over and over, to get me to give it up, to stick with Weddings by Woodwards. They even try to change my ideas. I think they feel I've somehow diminished their work because I chose to leave, to pursue something else."

"I see."

He didn't, but he would soon.

"The other Woodwards, my brothers Reese and Donovan, and my sister, Katie, all are a part of the company. So are my parents and, of course, my grandmother. If she'd had more than one son, he'd be part of it, too. And be happy to be there."

"So you're the odd man out."

She nodded, grateful he understood.

"That must make it very difficult for you, Sara."

"I manage." The empathy in his voice caught her attention. She tried to read his expression, but instead her attention snagged on the way his dark hair curled, ever so slightly, into his neck. Not long, but not really short, either. It suited him perfectly.

For half a second Sara wondered how it would feel to sift her fingers through those curls. She captured the errant thought by eating some salad and reminding herself she was here to plan a wedding, not to get sidetracked by a compassionate cowboy.

Maybe she'd said enough, maybe Cade would understand without further explanations of the ways her family would try to get her to stay.

As they shared their meal, dessert and coffee, Sara kept the discussion centered on the wedding. It was clear Cade had thought about it overnight because he made decisions that enabled Sara to check off several items on the long list of plans to be made, and add more after she'd paged through Karen's album.

"Well, that was productive." He grinned. "I never expected to get so much done over lunch. We should do this again."

Her heart wanted to agree, but her head reminded her that she was staying at her parents' house. Now they were back in town, she'd need to spend time with them. Besides, there was no way Sara could have lunch with him again without the family knowing and thinking something was happening between them.

Which it wasn't. Cade was nice, good-looking and comfortable to be around. But he was a client. Period.

"I'd like to see those pictures of outdoor weddings you talked about, Sara. I have an idea."

"Care to share?"

"Not yet." He shook his head. "It's still in the germination stage. I'm not certain it's viable. I'll do some checking on that this afternoon."

"Your ranch must be a well-oiled machine," she said, laying her napkin beside her plate. "You're lucky to be able to leave when you need to."

"I have very good hands and a foreman who knows the stock almost as well as I." He checked his watch. "But I should be getting back. If my predictions are accurate, I will have a mare foaling tonight."

"Isn't that out of season?"

"It happens. Have you ever seen a brand new colt, Sara?" She shook her head.

"You'll have to come out to the ranch, then. I'm kind of glad it's happened just now because your nephews will—"

"Cade! What did you think of my soup?" A tall, thin man with graying sideburns and wrapped in a pristine white apron clapped a hand on Cade's shoulder.

"Fantastic, Leon. As usual. This is Sara Woodward. She thought it was delicious, too. Sara, this is Chef Leon. He and his wife, Aimée, own Cartier's."

"My pleasure." Leon shook her hand gravely, but his eyes twinkled. "Don't hold my hand too long, my dear Sara. Aimée will make me scrub pots if she sees us."

Sara drew her hand away quickly, laughing at his silliness. "It's a pleasure to meet you, Chef. The whole meal was delicious."

"Sara tried to steal my sorbet. I gobbled it down too fast." Cade winked at her. "Any seconds?"

"One per customer," Leon said. "Even our friends must abide by Aimée's rules."

"I thought I'd find you here, Leon." A petite woman with a cloud of silver hair linked her arm through her husband's. "Cade, you are a bad influence. First my husband buys a horse which he cannot ride and now he tells me you talked him into going fishing on Sunday after church, our busiest time. I thought you were my friend."

"I am, Aimée." Cade rose, hugged her then sat down again. "Meet Sara."

"Hello. You have lovely hair, Sara. Mine is stick straight."

"Ah, my dear Aimée. You have other assets." Leon planted a light kiss on her cheek, his eyes glowing with love.

"I don't know what. I'm as plain as a pikestaff and I can't cook a thing." Aimée smiled, her face flushed with pleasure.

Leon slid his arm around her waist. "I didn't fall in love with your cooking, sweetheart."

Sara swallowed hard, trying to dissolve the lump in her

throat at the look the two exchanged. This was love, the kind of love that accepted the other person, warts and all. For a moment her heart bulged with envy for the other woman.

"It's a wonder you two get anything done with all this romantic stuff." Cade pretended to wince at Leon's cuff to his shoulder. "Is your birthday party still on, Aimée?"

"That's what Leo says, although I think it's wrong to close the restaurant for my fortieth birthday. I don't want to celebrate being forty!"

"We'll celebrate each year, darling," Leon told her, brushing her chin with his fingertip. "Every day with you is a gift from God. Now I must go before the kitchen falls apart." He strode across the room and through the swinging doors.

"Will you come to my party, Sara?"

"Oh." Sara blinked, surprised by the invitation. "It's very kind of you, but I'm—"

"Sara works for Woodwards. She probably has to check if the evening is free. But I'll bring her if she can come." Cade eased over the moment with smooth aplomb. "I have your gift all picked out, Aimée."

"As long as it isn't a horse to go with Leon's, I'll love it. I am not a horse person. But I have a soft spot for a certain rancher." Aimée hugged him, smiled at Sara and excused herself to speak to another customer.

"They seem like newlyweds." Sara studied the tiny woman. "Have they been married very long?"

"About twelve years, I guess." Cade swallowed the last of his coffee.

"Have they any children?" Sara wondered how anyone could run a place like this, with its extended hours, and manage children, as well.

"Aimée can't have children." Cade's voice dropped as he

shifted slightly forward, ensuring no one could overhear. "She had a very bad brush with cancer and—" He shrugged. "They both come from big families with lots of kids, so it's been rough. When Leon bought this place, they seemed to find their niches. She's the most perfect hostess."

Sara watched Aimée kneel down to speak to a little girl who was having lunch. Aimée's tender smile transformed her face and the child responded.

"Leon doesn't mind not being a father?" she asked as Aimée rose, stroked the girl's brown head then fished in her pocket for a treat.

Cade touched her hand, drawing her attention.

"Leon minds like crazy, Sara." He met her stare with a level look. "He used to work for my dad. Every year during foaling, all he could talk about was what he'd do when he became a daddy. But Leon didn't marry Aimée for children. He married her because he loves her, has since the day she ran into his precious car in high school."

The freedom of such love made Sara want to cry. Leon didn't think Aimée needed changing. He didn't want to make her into something else. He just loved her.

"They're very lucky," she whispered, her throat tight.

"It's not luck." Cade held her gaze with his own. "Leon believes that God knows what He's doing, that there is a reason he is not a parent. And he's learned to be content with that, to trust God."

"I guess that's one way to come to peace with his situation." Sara tried to break the visual connection between them but couldn't.

"That's not it." Cade frowned. "Leon has faith that there's a plan at work in this world and that plan is bigger than one man and one woman's wishes. He's relinquishing his own wants in favor of what God decides. It's trust."

"If you say so." Sara tore her gaze from his, fiddled with the edge of the tablecloth.

"You don't believe in God?"

His question pierced any pretense she might have mustered and went straight to the heart of the matter. But Sara was beginning to realize that Cade Porter was like that. He didn't play games, didn't wheedle and trick. He was honest and straightforward.

"Do you believe in God, Sara?"

And unrelenting.

"Oh, I think He's out there. Somewhere."

"But?"

"I don't think our personal issues matter much to God. I think He expects us to use our brains and manage on our own."

"Why do you think that?"

She couldn't answer. Not without revealing her own misfit status. If God cared so much, if He cared the way she'd been told He did, why couldn't she get in touch with Him? Why did she feel always on the outside of the faith circle, just as she did in her own family circle? Why did it always seem God shut out Sara Woodward?

She straightened. "I need to leave."

"Okay. I'll give you a ride back." He rose, held her chair then guided her to the front door.

Cade's immediate, nonchalant response shocked her, and truthfully, dismayed her. Which was ridiculous. Sara didn't want to debate God's love with Cade, so why should she feel so hurt that he didn't bother to question her on the subject?

"I had a reason for asking you here and for introducing you to my friends," he said as he helped her into his car. "I'd like to ask Leon and Aimée to cater Karen's wedding reception, whatever we decide it should be. Leon will love it. Karen worked for him once. After that lunch, I don't think you have any questions about his food."

"None." Sara waited until he was driving toward Woodwards. "You're already up to the reception, huh? You're really getting into wedding-planning mode." She giggled at his grimace. "If you keep this up, Grandma Winnie will want to hire you."

"And don't think I wouldn't be very good at my job." He pulled into a parking spot across from the store before turning to face her, his eyes crinkling at the corners as he grinned. "After you teach me the rest of it, that is."

"You, among the 'froufrou' of Woodwards?" She tipped her head to one side. "I can't quite imagine your fluffing the gowns."

Cade snorted.

"Ha! Not likely. First thing I'd do as your new employee is renovate that foyer. Get some serious man stuff in there."

Sara chuckled at the mental vision of Cade and her grandmother battling it out. But when he brushed his knuckles against the tip of her nose, the laughter died away. His blue eyes grew serious.

"We are not finished with our discussion about God, Sara," he warned softly. "It's simply been postponed for another time."

Cade was out of the car before she could respond. But Sara had already made up her mind. She wasn't going to debate God with him. In fact, she wasn't going to think about God at all.

A little voice inside her head laughed hilariously.

If she found success with that plan, maybe she could manage to stop thinking how handsome Cade Porter was and how being back in Denver wasn't turning out half as bad as she'd expected.

Chapter Four

"**I**'m really sorry about this, Cade."

Reese Woodward's sigh of regret transmitted clearly across the crackling phone line. Cade heard a thread of tiredness, too.

"Not a problem."

"For me it is. You can't know how good a day off would have felt today," Reese grumbled. "But with my grandmother out sick and Dad chasing down a fabric order in New York, I'm stuck filling in this afternoon. Good thing Sara's around to pitch in. In fact, she should be arriving at your place with the twins anytime now."

"We didn't have to do it today." Cade frowned.

Reese made it sound as if his sister had nothing better to do than act as a gofer and run errands. Sara had put her career on hold to come home, but evidently her brother didn't appreciate her sacrifice.

"I don't think the kids could wait any longer. Luckily, Sara's home. Even better, she's got the kind of job you can leave for a while."

As if her life would be waiting for her to pick it up when

Sara returned to L.A.? That sounded selfish. It bugged Cade to hear her dismissed so readily.

"I hope you'll be able to visit another time," was all he said.

"Count on it. I really want to thank you for doing this. The kids haven't been able to talk about anything else since you promised them a ride."

"It's my pleasure. They'll be in good hands."

"All of them?" Reese hinted, innuendo veiling his tone.

"Don't worry, your sister will be fine, too, if that's really worrying you. Talk to you soon." Cade hung up, irritated by the muffled laughter.

Seeing Reese peer through the coffee-shop window had seemed funny at first. After all, Cade had done the same thing to Karen once—and lived to regret it. But after Cade had driven Winifred and Sara home, Winifred had given him a very smug look. And now Reese was hinting at something.

What was it Sara had said about her family? They overruled her decisions?

Cade's momentary puzzlement evaporated as the object of his thoughts pulled into his yard, toddlers at either side in the backseat, faces pressed to the window. He walked across the graveled driveway and pulled open Sara's door.

"Hello." His breath stopped at her beauty, fully exposed now that glossy curls had been drawn away from her face into a ponytail of ringlets. "Welcome to my ranch."

"Cade, it's beautiful." She stepped out and stood for several moments, heedless of the children's demands for release. She surveyed craggy peaks with the jutting hoods of snow, the orange- and red-leafed quilts of color dotting the hillsides, the green carpeted paddocks sprawling around them. Finally she sighed. "It takes my breath away."

His, too, but that had nothing to do with the ranch.

"You're going to have a riot on your hands if we don't let those two out."

She glanced over one shoulder, blinked.

"Oops! That wasn't very doting aunt of me. Come on, guys. Settle down until I get you out of these seats."

Cade paused only a moment to see how she undid the buckles before opening the door on the far side and freeing the other twin.

"Welcome to my ranch, Brett." He set the sturdy feet on the ground, proudly relishing the boy's gaping stare.

"You can tell them apart?" Sara velvet eyes widened. "Nobody can tell them apart."

"Why not? Brett's the leader, typical first kid. He rushes into things. Brady holds back a bit to see what happens to Brett before he charges ahead. See?"

Brett flopped onto the ground and rolled down the nearest hill right into a patch of dried-up beans Cade's housekeeper hadn't yet harvested. Brady waited about five seconds before following suit.

"Maybe I should—"

Cade touched her arm, smiled.

"They're fine, Sara. They're working off some of that nonstop energy, which is a good thing. We'll call them back in a minute, okay?"

"Okay." She studied him for a second before her gaze slipped back to the boys.

"Do you ride much?"

"Me?" That got her attention. The blond ponytail wagged from side to side as she shook her head. "Never. I'm not—good with animals."

"Nonsense. My horses are very gentle. I'll teach you."

"I think you'll have your hands full with the boys." She grinned as the stocky-legged twins trudged up the hill toward them. "You two have been here ten minutes, and you're already filthy."

The boys ignored her.

"Horsie?" Brett asked, peering up at him.

"How about a baby horse first?" Cade looked to Sara for permission.

"Oh, your colt's been born? Yes, we'd love to see. Boys, you have to—"

He cut her off. "Let me play the bad guy. Okay?"

Sara blinked, shrugged. "Sure."

Cade crouched down to explain about the colt and the rules of the barn.

"His mama doesn't like anyone to touch her baby right now, but if you promise to be very quiet, we'll take a look." He couldn't help wondering where the twins' mother was, but now wasn't the time to ask. "Will you promise not to scare them?"

The boys nodded solemnly, then marched beside him, obviously curious but respecting what he'd said about following rules. Hiding his smile, Cade slid back the solid gate so they could peer through the bars into the stall where his newest animal stood beside its mother. Of his three guests, Sara seemed the most enthralled.

Her eyes glistened as mother and baby nuzzled each other. When the colt came close to sniff the treat Cade held out, Sara's fingers itched to slip between the bars to brush against its glossy mane.

"Beautiful," she whispered.

"Me!"

At the sharp cry, the colt jerked away and hid behind its mother, who made her displeasure clear.

"I want to touch it!"

"Brett." Cade got down level with the petulant boy, kept

his voice soft but firm. "When you yell like that, you scare the horses. They don't like it and they won't let you near them. You have to use your quietest voice. Remember what I said?"

"Sorry." The sadness on that little face reached deep down and squeezed his heart.

"You'll do better next time."

"Come on, let's leave them alone now," Sara murmured, one hand resting on each small shoulder.

"Don't want to." Brett dug in his heels.

"We might come back later, if you remember the rules. Rules are important when you're around horses." Cade explained how baby animals were always protected, just like little boys were. The twins understood that. They stepped backward respectfully as he shifted the stall door. He was inordinately pleased when Sara lingered for one last glance over the top. "Seen enough?"

"Yes. Sorry." She hurried past him, head down.

"Not a problem. We'll go this way now." He shepherded the kids to another part of the barn, wondering what he'd done to make her avoid him.

"Look, Auntie Sara!" After the first squeak, Brady's voice dropped to a whisper. "More babies."

The kids flopped to the floor to admire the litter of pups born to Cade's herding dog a few weeks ago. Sara kneeled beside them, stopping curious fingers when necessary. Cade didn't interfere because the dog was an experienced mom and although she kept a close eye on her pups, she didn't seem to mind the exuberant boys.

"We want a dog, Auntie Sara."

"You'll have to ask—" At that moment one of the pups crawled up her leg and tumbled into her lap. "Oh." Sara's velvet eyes begged him to help.

"It's okay." Cade hunkered down beside her. "You can pick it up."

She cupped her hands and he set the tiny body in her palms. She held it for a moment with such a tender look on her face that Cade found it hard to swallow past the lump blocking his throat.

"It's so precious," she whispered. "A tiny miracle of life."

The twins, picking up on her awe, touched the pup's head with reverence. Sara allowed them to hold the furry ball, but kept her palm underneath to protect it. Cade's throat tightened while his heart cried out.

This is what I want, God. A family to share my life.

The plea died a silent death as he fought back his own desire. He'd accepted God's will. He didn't need another lesson on loss.

Finally Sara set the puppy back beside its mother and drew the boys away.

"You came for a horse ride, remember?" The reminder quieted any argument the twins might have offered.

Cade led all three through the barn to the riding stable. At a prearranged signal, two of his precious miniatures were led inside.

"Baby horsies!" After a glance at Cade, Brett managed to control his voice but his face exposed his excitement.

"They're not colts," Cade explained to Sara. "They are mature now. This is as large as they get. Perfect for little ones to ride."

"Yes, they are." Her eyes glittered with pleasure as she carefully stroked one hand over the horse's flanks.

Cade introduced his youngest hand, a high-school student named Mark. Together they demonstrated how the saddles and harnesses worked. When he was certain the twins were comfortable around the animals, Cade asked Brady to get on the step.

"Why?" The boy looked toward Brett, his hesitation obvious.

"Because that's how you get on. This horse is called Rusty. He's going to take you for a ride now."

"Oh." Brady wordlessly beseeched Sara, and she immediately stepped forward.

"Come on, sweetie. Mark's going to stay right beside you. He won't let you fall." She shared a smile with Cade before she turned back to the child. "I'll be here, too. Isn't it fun?"

"Uh-huh." Brady glanced at his brother, who still stood on the ground. "Isn't Brett going?"

"In a minute," Cade assured him. He'd deliberately chosen to teach the more rambunctious boy himself so as to allow Sara to reassure Brady, if he needed it. He watched Brady climb on and settle. Satisfied when Mark had things well in hand, he turned to the other child. "Ready, Brett?"

"Yes."

Brady seemed amazed that his horse should be called Lulu and kept repeating it over and over. Both children caught on quickly, easily mastering how to direct their mounts. At one point, Cade turned his head and caught Sara watching him. She blushed before hiding behind the camera she'd brought to video the boys for Reese to watch later.

When Brady drooped in his seat, Cade gauged the twins had ridden long enough and signaled Mark. Sara put away her camera and hurried over to help. Brett kicked up a fuss until he caught Cade's frown and remembered the rules.

"Are those horses going outside now?" he asked.

Cade explained how the horses needed currying and a special treat for allowing themselves to be ridden. The boys took turns brushing, erupting into giggles when the horses snitched the carrots Mark had tucked into his back pockets. When Lulu nuzzled Cade's shirt pocket, looking for a sugar lump, even Sara laughed. Cade thought he could listen to that sound for a very long time.

"What do you say, guys?" Sara smiled benevolently when the twins obediently thanked him for the ride. "Very good," she praised.

"Can we ride Rusty and Lulu again?"

"You'll have to ask your dad," he said, dazzled by Sara's beauty. "Right now it's lunchtime. Let's go wash up. Mrs. Brown makes the best soup you've ever tasted."

"You don't have to feed them, Cade. The ride was more than enough."

Cade said nothing for a moment, enjoying watching the pair race across the grass toward the house. One look at Sara's face told him she'd grab any excuse to stuff the kids in the car and leave. He didn't understand why, only that he didn't want her to go.

Not yet.

"Don't spoil my fun. Please? I got the miniatures because I thought one day my own k— It's been a long time since I've laughed so hard. I don't want it to end yet." He wondered if she'd noticed his slip and change midstream.

Sara chewed her bottom lip but finally nodded.

"Okay, lunch. Alhough I'm pretty sure you'll wish you hadn't offered after watching them eat." Her whole face lit up with a saucy grin. "Be warned, your housekeeper may quit because of us. Brett, leave that cat alone." She widened her eyes. "See? You'll be so tired of us, you'll sleep for ages."

Tired—of this? Not in a lifetime. In fact, for the first time in months, the ranch seemed alive with laughter and joy, the sound of a family.

Cade cut short the thought.

They weren't his family. That could never be.

But surely God wouldn't mind if he pretended for a little while.

* * *

"Are you sure Mrs. Brown doesn't mind watching them while we're gone? She's older than me, and I get winded after ten minutes." Sara paused to study the exterior of the big rambling farmhouse. The fresh paint and other details made it looked loved and welcoming.

"She adores kids, but don't let that doting smile fool you. She can be a tartar." Cade made a face. "I should know. She's been here so long she thinks she's the boss."

Sara chuckled out loud. That cowboy charm was hard to resist.

"She's a great cook. The boys' mom used to make soup like that."

"She doesn't now?"

"Taylor died a couple of years ago. Accident on an icy road. It's been hard on Reese." Sara inhaled and counted the aromas. Freshly cut pine for a fire, wood smoke curling upward in a gray spiral beyond a distant hill, dried pasture grasses. "You must love it here. Peace and quiet, beauty."

And freedom. Nobody watching every move, checking on you, second-guessing your decisions.

"I do love it. It gets lonely sometimes, but I go over to the bunkhouse and the guys soon cure me." He pointed to a long narrow building set in a glade well away from the house and the barns. "They have windows and a patio on the valley side so they can relax when work's over for the day without feeling overlooked."

"Is that what you wanted to show me?" His request that she linger after lunch had surprised Sara, adding to her curiosity when he claimed he needed her opinion.

"No, that isn't it. We're going for a walk, if you can manage it in those shoes." He glanced down, frowned. "At least they don't have spike heels."

"They're very comfortable," she assured him. "I can walk wherever you want."

"Don't you have a pair of boots?"

"No. It doesn't rain that much in—" She glanced at his face and knew she was off-track. "Oh. You mean, cowboy boots?"

"Is there another kind?" he asked with a smirk.

"I don't have any cowboy boots."

"That's too bad. They're the most comfortable things you'll ever wear."

Sara doubted that. His pointed toes didn't look any more comfortable than the fashionable shoes Katie loved. But she said nothing, trying to match his stride as they moved laterally away from the house and up the slow incline between perfectly spaced rows of evergreens.

"This looks like a Christmas tree forest."

"Nope, although we do have some land for that."

"Is it some kind of hiking trail?"

"Nope."

"Now I'm really curious." Sara drew fresh air into her lungs as she trod the last few yards up the hill. At the top she held her breath, transfixed by what she saw.

A small white octagon with windows on every side sat perched on a craggy point.

"It's lovely. What is it?"

"It was my grandmother's painting house. My grandfather built it for her. Come, I'll show you." It seemed perfectly normal when his fingers grasped hers, drawing her up the gravel path to a set of glass doors which swung wide-open at his touch. "She used to paint here. If it was windy or wet or cold, she could sit inside and still have an unobstructed view."

Canvases leaned their faces against one wall. Nearby, in a tiny kitchen, tubes of paints and brushes lay in neat rows on granite surfaces. Sara caught her breath.

"Emily Porter," she breathed, recognizing a small watercolor in a frame by the door. She turned to stare at him. "She was your grandmother?"

"Yes." He drew her farther inside. "She used to bring me here sometimes. She'd give me paper, paints, a brush, tell me to look around and put what I saw on the paper." Cade made a face. "I wasn't very good, although she never said so."

He kept speaking, but Sara didn't hear. Every sense locked on the panoramic vista before her. As if drawn by a powerful magnet, she opened two doors and stepped onto a cedar balcony overlooking a valley and the rugged Rockies beyond.

"It's fantastic."

"Kind of gives you a new appreciation for God, doesn't it?" Cade's voice came from behind her left shoulder, low, personal. "What kind of mind could create this beauty from nothing? I never get tired of imagining how God thinks."

Sara didn't want to talk about God.

"It's a fantastic workspace." Spying clay figures on a table in the corner, she walked to them and traced one finger over the smooth hardened face of a younger Cade. "I didn't know she also sculpted."

"She'd just begun when the arthritis took over. I was bored last winter when we kept having those ice storms, so I bought some clay. Thought I'd try my hand at it, see if I could give up ranching for a more lucrative career." He lifted a plastic sheet for her inspection, grinned at her gurgled laugh and shrugged. "I'm worse at it than painting, so I guess I'll stick with ranching."

Say something nice, Sara.

"Um, what was it going to be?"

"Karen."

"Ah." Since Sara could find nothing in the misshapen lump that resembled humanity, she opted for a change of subject.

Hard plastic shells with indentations of a nose, eyes and lips were lined up across a counter. "What are these?"

"Hockey masks. I hoped to learn to sculpt faces from them."

Sara touched another of his attempts, struggling to suppress her amusement.

"Go ahead, make fun of me. I don't have a lot of patience when it comes to this stuff," he said, one red spot highlighting each cheekbone as he poked at the hardened bits of clay.

"I see that."

"I suppose you could do better."

He was pushing her buttons and Sara knew it, but she'd never been able to resist a challenge.

"Do you have any clay left?"

Without speaking, he opened a cupboard, hefted a big box onto the counter.

"Help yourself. It should still be usable. I wrapped it pretty tight."

Sara lifted away the layers of plastic and dug her fingers into the dull gray mass, mentally searching for an idea. A sketch, probably Emily's, of a child in a cape jumping from a boulder sat nearby. That brought to mind the twins and their love of dress-up. Quickly she manipulated the earth into a small mask and added enough details to give it a frog-like appearance. Brady's favorite animal.

"Show-off." Cade leaned over her shoulder, his face near hers as he studied her work. "Okay, you're way better than me. I guess you best make something for Brett while you're at it."

"How did you know this was for Brady?"

"Your face." Cade laughed at her moue of disgust. "When you're concentrating, your forehead wrinkles up the same way his does."

"Such a lavish compliment."

"Also, he told me he loves frogs."

"Love is an understatement." She pinched out a tiger face for Brett. But after a while she realized that Cade was watching her, not her hands, and that made her nervous. She finished as quickly as she could.

"Amazing."

"It's rough. The twins are probably causing problems for your housekeeper." She closed the box securely, then scrubbed her hands clean in the nearby sink. "I must stop playing and get back to my job of babysitting."

"Your special-effects work—" Cade's pensive gaze rested on the masks. "Have you done a lot of it?"

"Hardly any. I'm hoping to put together a portfolio to impress Gideon Glen. Have you heard of him?"

"Genius of special effects. Who hasn't?"

"I want to apprentice with him." She studied the two masks, knew they were too rough. "The problem is there is never enough time and no place to work. I was going to use Dad's workshop while they were away, but now—"

Better not to explain that even if her father would allow it, the rest of the family always found something else for her to do.

"You're welcome to come out here, use my grandmother's studio whenever you like. In fact, I'd be glad if you did. It seems a shame to waste the place."

Sara blinked, surprised by the offer.

"That's nice of you, but I can't afford to rent," she explained. "I'm still paying for my place in L.A., and it's not cheap there."

"I didn't mean rent it. I meant use it. For free." Cade's blue stare held her motionless. "Well, sort of free."

Another person who had plans for her.

The radio at his waist crackled. Cade snapped it on, responded and listened as Mrs. Brown told him the boys' DVD was finished and she was serving milk and cookies.

"Thanks. We'll be right there." He opened a drawer and pulled out a sheet of plastic which he carefully tucked around the two masks Sara had made. "This will keep them from drying out until you can come back and work on them again."

"It's really nice of you, Cade, but I don't think—"

"I'm hoping you might repay me in another way."

"How?" She followed him out of the studio, waiting until he'd closed and locked all the doors.

"I'm on the board of the children's hospital. We're working on fund-raising to add a wing which will work with kids who've been maimed or otherwise injured and need rehab. Your masks—" he jerked a thumb over one shoulder as they walked downhill toward the main house "—gave me an idea."

"Uh-oh."

"There's a newcomer at our church, Olivia Hastings, who volunteers with a local little theater group. She has a great idea for a dinner theater production we could use as a fund-raiser. But she insists she can't do it without help, specifically special effects. You and she need to talk."

"Cade, I do makeup. I've never actually done special effects before."

"But if you did something for Olivia's play, wouldn't that give you at least a start on the portfolio you need to work with this fellow?"

"Well—" Sara stopped, stunned by the possibilities of what he was suggesting. When she looked up, Cade was smiling.

"I think God brought you home for a reason, Sara. To help out your family, yes. But maybe He also intended this to be a time for you, a chance to try something new. It would be just like God to arrange it so you could help the hospital while helping yourself."

"I can't imagine God—"

"Don't say no. Not yet." The persuasion in his voice intensified. "Will you at least think about talking to Olivia? You could use the studio whenever you liked and your work wouldn't be in anyone's way."

God? Could it really be His doing?

All things work together for good—Winnie's favorite verse echoed in her mind, a memory long forgotten.

Part of Sara yearned to believe that God had organized this homecoming especially for her benefit, that He cared about her enough to create a specially designed plan that would allow her to reach the goal she'd dreamed about since high school.

But inside a whispering voice reminded her that she'd trusted God before and been disappointed.

"Will you at least meet with her to talk about it?" he pressed.

It was tempting, so tempting to grab the chance to focus on her own goals, especially in Cade's inspiring studio.

"I thought we were supposed to be planning your sister's wedding."

Cade's grin split his face. He tilted his head at a cocky angle and winked at her.

"I'm not just a dumb rancher, you know. I've got an idea. We could hold the wedding there, inside Grandmother's studio." His face came alive as he spoke. "Karen won't want a huge wedding, so I'm sure the building could accommodate everyone. If she was married in the evening, we could have a candlelight walk up the hill."

Her brain caught his train of thought and created a romantic world.

"The ceremony would be on the balcony with the stars as a backdrop. Leon could set up a buffet lunch afterward and folks could mingle and talk, sit outside."

"Keep talking."

"If it's nice, tables outside. If not, we'll use the inside. Maybe we'd even have some fireworks. What do you think?"

His word picture was every bit as vivid as his grandmother's paintings. Until reality hit.

"What if it's wintertime when Karen comes home?"

It should have dampened his enthusiasm, but instead Cade's face grew more animated. His blue eyes expanded, darkened. To Sara's shock, he reached out and hugged her.

"Yes! I should have thought of that. Thank you."

"For what? What did I do?" She hurried to keep up as he moved toward the house. Before he pulled open the door, she grabbed his arm. "Cade?"

"My parents were married on New Year's Eve, Sara, on that very hilltop, in an old barn that used to stand there. Their reception turned into a New Year's Eve party the community talked about for ages." His smile blazed. "I have no doubt Karen will love that date. And she's sure to be home before then."

Sara gulped. There was one week left in October. A New Year's wedding left a mere nine weeks, including Thanksgiving, to plan an event for the busiest night of the year. And that didn't account for the possibility of bad weather, transportation out to the ranch or accommodation for the guests.

But if she could pull it off—

Sara's fingers curled around the newel and she hung on, forcing air in and out of her lungs as she considered the implications. She was the junior employee, hadn't done a wedding for ages. She might have to ask the family's help. That meant they'd come out here, see her work and know she was putting together a portfolio.

But you'd have time to create that portfolio.

Yes, but the family would all show up with differing opinions of how things should look and they'd ride roughshod over her work, probably interfere in the play, too.

But if you don't take this opportunity, if you don't at least try to push forward, you'll never achieve your dream.

Her stomach heaved at the possibilities. The world tilted.

The house door burst open. Brett stuck out his head.

"Auntie Sara, I don't feel good."

Sara glanced from his green-tinged countenance to Cade's beaming one.

Everything grew blurry. Her stomach danced a jig.

"It must be contagious," she said right before everything went black.

Chapter Five

Cade watched thick golden lashes flutter and lift.

"Stay still, Sara. You fainted. Don't sit up until you feel ready."

"The kids," she whispered, then licked her lips as if she'd left the desert. "What about the twins?"

"Mark and Mrs. Brown are watching them jump on the trampoline." He read the question in her eyes. "Karen loved gymnastics. I never got rid of it."

"Oh. I thought Brett was sick." She inched upright on the sofa, her skin less pale against her orange T-shirt than it had been when she'd melted into a puddle on his doorstep.

"He *was* sick. Now he's fine. That's boys for you. Let me help." Cade stuffed pillows behind her back, offered her the glass of ice water Mrs. Brown had left.

"Thanks," she whispered.

"You're welcome. Do you faint often?"

"I've never done it before. I guess I hurried down that hill too fast, trying to keep up." The husky edge to her voice diminished. She sipped a few more drops of the water, rubbed her scalp under the ponytail. "I'm sorry."

"For what?"

"Causing all this trouble." Her cheeks grew pinker.

"You hardly passed out on purpose. Not that it was any trouble. You don't weigh more than a feather."

"You carried me in?"

"Had to get you inside." He shrugged. "No big deal."

"Oh. Well, thanks anyway." She avoided him by glancing around the room. A tiny frown rippled her forehead.

"What's wrong?" Cade glanced around, noticed nothing amiss.

"I'd never have pegged you as ultramodern." Her nose wrinkled with distaste as she surveyed the chrome and leather furniture in the room.

"Oh." He'd forgotten the impact of all that red. "Marnie was redoing the house."

"I see."

There it was again, that knowing glint that feathered through her sympathetic brown gaze. Suddenly he recognized that Sara Woodward only looked like she wore her emotions on her sleeve. There was so much more inside.

"You haven't been in here recently, have you, Cade?"

"Why do you say that?"

"It looks unlived in."

"I prefer my study."

"I understand." Her mouth curved in a gentle smile that said she thought he found the room too vivid a reminder of what he'd lost. It wasn't totally accurate, but she didn't need to know the sad details of his life.

"Tell me something," he asked without thinking. "Why did you choose to work with makeup?"

Sara wiggled against her cushions, head bent. But after a moment she finally looked at him again, barriers up.

"Why not?"

Cade opened his mouth to respond but she didn't give him a chance.

"My family doesn't understand why, either. I can't really explain it to them except—it's like creating a mask. Makeup lets you be who you want. A few adjustments and a face can go from ecstasy to craziness." She shrugged. "Maybe it's a way of hiding from life."

Cade grimaced. "Sounds painful."

"But freeing. Life's like that sometimes."

He had a hunch Sara was not only talking about her work. The hint underlying her softly whispered words said more than she realized and probably way more than she intended.

"How did you get started?"

"It's a long story."

"I've got time."

"Oh, well." Sara closed her eyes, smiled. "My grandfather was known for making very intricate and beautiful porcelain faces. He was determined to be a toymaker, so he left his home and his family to make his name. I always felt like a misfit, so I guess I identified pretty heavily with him."

"I'd like to meet him."

"He died right after my dad was born. Anyway, I figured I was like him and that's why I never fit in with my family. I had a job at Woodwards on Saturdays when I was in high school. I started plastering makeup on the old mannequins." She laughed. "Horrible at first, but I got better. One evening a bride needed help and I was the only one left. Winnie asked me if I could do anything. The next day she enrolled me in a cosmetology school."

"You must have done a good job on the bride."

"She was lovely to begin with. I didn't do much." Again the slim shoulders lifted. "I think my grandmother assumed I'd come back to Woodwards after training. But I got a taste of theatrical work and loved it. Makeup was something all mine, something I could pour my heart and soul into." Her voice faded away, eyes shadowed with past memories. "Theater work taught me the art of pretense, how to hide feelings or exaggerate them with makeup or masks or grease-paint. I was hooked."

Cade's curiosity about this woman grew with every word.

"I've bored you to silence. Sorry." A quiet sadness chased away her radiance. "When it comes to my work, I forget not everyone is as enthusiastic as me."

"Don't apologize for loving what you do." The wistfulness of her expression had him reaching to cover her hand with his. "When it's your passion, it's hard not to be enthusiastic, isn't it?"

Sara's gaze slid from his face to their hands. She carefully drew hers away, ostensibly to get a tissue. But that was an excuse and Cade knew it. She didn't like his touch.

"What made you think you were like your grandfather?"

"In my senior year I read my grandfather's diaries. I never knew him, but the way he wrote about his toymaking, the zeal he felt in forming the clay into faces for the dolls he'd envisioned—that intrigued me because I found the same thing with makeup." Sara shrugged. "What's your passion?" she asked, turning the focus on him.

Family.

How could he explain his longing for a circle of loved ones? Cade ached for the hugs and tears, the teasing, the laughter, even the disagreements that happened between people who had confidence that no matter what, the ones who counted would always be there for him.

His worst fear was that after Karen married she'd want to live somewhere other than the ranch. Then his dream of a family would die. Just as the dream of having children had.

But as he stared into Sara's wide glowing eyes, Cade knew he couldn't say it. She wouldn't understand why family was so important to him, not without hearing a lot of his history, and even if she wanted to listen, he didn't want to review the painful past.

"I tend to ramble about the ranch," he temporized. "A stallion I'm working with, a mare that's ready to foal, a colt that shows promise. I get carried away, don't even notice how glazed-over the stares have become until the person I'm talking to makes some excuse and leaves."

"It's really embarrassing when they leave," Sara agreed solemnly. Her generous lips quirked up in a smirk that revealed a delightful dimple.

"It's way worse when you meet them on the street and they take off in the opposite direction before you've even opened your mouth." How long had it been since he'd had a silly conversation like this?

Answer: too long.

"Don't take this the wrong way, but I really should go. I can't imagine why Reese hasn't phoned to demand an explanation." Sara swung her legs off the sofa, paused. "Or maybe I can." She sighed heavily.

"I wish you'd explain that." Cade shook his head when she began to make an excuse. "I saw the way your grandmother was acting the other day, Sara. And this morning Reese hinted at something. I'd like to understand what's going on."

Sara took a long time to decide, her pensive face scrutinizing every detail of his before she finally nodded.

"They have designs on you," she muttered as a quick flush of red surged up to color her cheeks.

"Designs? That sounds so—melodramatic." Cade struggled to hide his laughter. "Who does?"

"My family. Particularly my grandmother." Her fingers

played with the afghan he'd laid over her legs when he'd first carried her in. After a moment she peeked up from between her lashes. "But also Katie, Reese. My parents."

"Why?" He listened as she explained the aftermath of his phone call to Katie the day they'd gone for lunch. With every word she confirmed the suspicions that had hidden in the recesses of his mind.

Her family was matchmaking.

"You don't believe me." Sara rose, folded the afghan and set it on the sofa. She smoothed her sweater over her hips, raked a hand through the few tendrils of gold that had escaped her ponytail. "Never mind. I'd better collect the boys and leave. Thanks for the ride."

"Wait!" Cade jumped up, blocked her way out. "I believe you, Sara. I suspected something along the same lines myself. But I don't think it's as bad as you imagine. Are you saying they seriously think they can throw us together and we'll—stick?"

She nodded her head.

"After one meeting?"

"This is four. And they think big."

"But surely you must have told them otherwise?" He gulped. "Didn't you?"

A half smile played with her lips.

"They don't listen to me. They never have."

"Because?"

"I'm the baby of the family. I'm too young, naive, dumb—put in whatever word you like. They know best and they're determined to see I get it—whether I want it or not." Mischief added texture to the richness of her eyes. "What's best for me, they think, is to stay at Woodwards. I'm sort of an oddball in my family."

What character she had, to be able to laugh at what had to be a painful situation.

"Oddball?"

"That sounds self-indulgent. It's more like I don't fit the pattern they want for me. I never have. Top it off with my leaving to have a career outside of Woodwards and—" She left it hanging, her head tilted to one side.

"So to get you to stay, they'll try to pair you up. With me." She nodded.

"But—"

"They think if they can get us interested in each other, I'll change my plans."

"No offense, but it's not going to happen. I'll never get married."

To his surprise, Sara nodded.

"You keep saying that, Cade. Repeat it whenever you meet any member of my family." She turned her head toward the window as Brett's yelp sounded. "I have to go. Thanks for everything. I'd like to help your friend Olivia, but I don't think it's a good idea for me to come out here, even if it is only to work."

"Because your family will assume something else is going on?" He frowned at her nod. "Are you sure you haven't misunderstood, Sara? I mean, sure, they're concerned for your future, but actually finding you a husband? It's—"

"True. I'll prove it. Phone the store on Monday. Tell Katie you want someone else. Say I don't have enough experience, or my ideas are nuts. Whatever. Then wait." She stepped past him and out of the living room, her nose wrinkling as she avoided the massive metal sculpture Marnie had loved. "I guarantee they'll find a reason you and I have to work together."

"But I don't want someone else to organize Karen's wedding. You've got all the good ideas."

"Thank you," she said quietly, her eyes suddenly shiny. "That's very kind. But you have no idea what they're like.

Reese was watching us at the coffee shop. Know why? He was checking you out before he gave the family a report on our, er, compatibility."

Embarrassment vied with irritation. The latter won.

"I don't care." Cade followed her out of the room. "Let them assume whatever they want. Why is it up to us to stop their speculation?"

Sara stopped so quickly he almost bumped into her. She faced him, her eyes narrowed.

"Huh?"

"We can't stop anyone from making assumptions. You've never been able to stop it, have you?" When she shook her head, he continued. "Okay. So let's ignore it. It doesn't matter what they do anyway because a wedding's not in my future—except for Karen's."

At least he'd gotten that out of the way so she wouldn't expect anything.

"Not fighting it will only encourage them," Sara warned.

"So? You and I know the truth. We've got some great ideas going for Karen. You could make a big difference in the hospital's theater production and by so doing achieve some of your own goals. Are you going to let them interfere with that?"

"I'm not sure—"

"How badly do you want this dream you've been talking about, Sara?" Cade held his breath as he watched emotions flicker across her expressive face.

Sara said nothing. But her whole body underwent a transformation. Her eyes began to glow, her shoulders pressed up with her straightening spine. Her chin lifted, thrust forward. Even the orange of her shirt seemed to intensify.

"You want a chance with Gideon Glen, don't you? So take one. Insist on spending time doing what you need to grab your chance at special effects." Cade softened his words. "You're not responsible for what they think, Sara, only for what you do."

After a yawning silence, she nodded.

"Okay."

"Fantastic!" The board was going to thank him mightily. "There's a fund-raising meeting tomorrow afternoon, after church. Can you make it?"

"Yes." No hesitation now. "I'll also begin putting things for the wedding together now that we know where it's taking place. Can you stop by the store Monday afternoon to go over things with me?"

"Yes." Cade grinned at her, a coconspirator in her quest for freedom from the family he wished was his. How stupid was that?

"I'm sorry you got caught up in their games, Cade," Sara apologized quietly. "It's embarrassing for me and you're making it easier, which is very nice. But be warned, you will be in the thick of things. They'll probably take up your time trying to sing my praises."

"I already know you're smart and giving and that you have enough courage to stand up to strong personalities." He smiled. "Nobody's going to change my opinion of you, Sara. But they won't talk me into a relationship other than friendship, so stop worrying."

He walked her out to the car, helped her buckle the kids into their seats.

"Why not marriage, if you don't mind my asking?" She leaned against the car, her stare steady. "I mean, you've intimated several times that you're committed to being single. But you talk about family with great feeling. You're good with kids. Why are you so against getting married?"

He owed her honesty.

"I'm not. But marriage isn't God's will for me. I'd prefer otherwise, but remember what I told you about Leon?"

Her golden brows drew together. "Sort of."

"I share his belief that God has a certain path marked out for me and that my job is to follow it. When Marnie died, God made it clear that marriage is not His choice for me. I trust that He has a reason for that and since I gave Him my life, I'll obey His will."

"As simple as that?"

He laughed while inside his soul begged for courage.

"It's not simple at all. Giving up my will is the hardest thing I've ever done. But it is what God asks of me and I know it's for the best. The promise is *All things work together for those who love God.* God always honors His promises, Sara."

She remained quiet for several moments, studying the earth. When she lifted her head, her eyes shone like polished obsidian. She was weeping—for him?

"I'm doubly grateful you're willing to help me, Cade, knowing how you feel and how my family will put pressure on you to change your mind. Thank you."

"You're welcome."

It wasn't until after her car disappeared, when his housekeeper had left and the hands were busy with their own lives that Cade appreciated how much Sara Woodward was going to count on him to reach for her dream. He'd volunteered to stand between her and her family. But around her, the yearning for those precious bonds grew.

"Am I doing the right thing, Lord?"

No still small voice told him to back down, so Cade grew more comfortable with his decision. Those melting brown eyes had burned a place in his brain. Cade would be there for Sara, as long as she needed him.

Whatever it cost him.

* * *

On Friday night Sara threw caution to the wind and dressed up, including heels, for her grandmother's birthday.

"You look lovely tonight."

She caught her breath at the familiar voice. She turned a little too quickly, grabbed Cade's arm to steady herself.

"Thank you." In fact, Cade looked fantastic in his black suit and pristine white shirt. "So do you. But what are you doing here?"

"Bringing birthday greetings to your grandmother. She insisted I come, said you didn't have a date and it would be awkward for you."

"Oh." Anger ripped through her. "I'm so sorry, Cade. She had no right. Tonight was your boys' group thing, wasn't it? Surely you didn't cancel for this?"

He shook his head.

"Change of plans. We're doing a hike, a wiener roast and some kite flying tomorrow afternoon."

"Tomorrow's the first of November. Our first rehearsal for the fund-raiser. You'll miss it." Funny how strong the sense of loss rushing through her. Cade had gone to great lengths to get the play up and running. "I'm sorry Grandmother interfered. I'll speak to her."

"Don't bother." He lifted two glasses of punch off a passing tray, handed one to her. "I think talking to her will only make it worse. About the play—congratulations on taking the first step toward your goal." He chinked his glass against hers, blue eyes twinkling. "How does it feel?"

"Terrifying. Exciting. Like I've stepped on a runaway train." She sipped some of the fizzy ginger ale and juice concoction. "There's a lot of work to do. But it's so much fun."

"Cade, my dear. I'm so glad you came to be with Sara. She was looking awfully lonely all by herself."

"Grandmother, you had no right to ask Cade to change his plans."

"I'm sure he's allowed to miss the occasional meeting."

Winnie's nonchalance floored Sara, but she had no time to protest before Cade intervened.

"Happy birthday, Mrs. Woodward. I hope you have many more." He held out a small silver box. "With my best wishes."

"Why thank you, my dear. Now what can this be?" Winnie sank onto a chair, fingers curling around the bow as eagerly as a child's on Christmas morning.

Sara met Cade's gaze. He was so good at hiding his emotions. At the moment he even looked as if he was enjoying himself.

"It's lovely." Winnie lifted a silver filigree butterfly out of the box and held it on the end of her finger as if waiting for it to fly away. "Thank you, dear boy." She rose on tiptoe and pressed a kiss against his cheek before pinning the gift against her black silk gown.

"It's very pretty," Sara agreed, wondering how he'd known her grandmother preferred silver jewelry to gold.

"Wear it in health. I hope you're feeling better?"

"It's early days, the doctors say. Not much change yet. But I press on. What did you two young things have your heads together about?" Winnie asked coyly, her eyes moving from Sara to Cade in a suggestive way.

Sara wished she could sink through the floor, but of course Woodwards would never own a building with a weak floor, particularly not in the ballroom.

"My sister's wedding, of course." Cade's smooth tone defied contradiction. "What else would we have to talk about, Mrs. Woodward?"

He was good. If it hadn't been for the wink he sent her behind Winnie's back, Sara would have bought his nonchalance. Unfortunately her mother had seen the wink and was now grinning like a wise cat.

"Sara's come up with some great ideas. But it's a lot of work. Every time I turn around there's something else to think about. I have to get her help with so many details. Thank the Lord she's good at what she does."

"Yes, thank Him." Grandma Winnie didn't look quite so smug. She turned to Sara. "What's this I hear about some children's hospital?"

"Cade suggested I use my skills to help with their fundraising event. Perhaps Woodwards could contribute, Grandmother?"

"Naturally. But, dear, are you sure you can spare the time? After all, as Cade says, getting his wedding organized is your top priority."

"My sister's wedding. I will never be a groom," Cade told her, his voice firm, cool. "But surely your granddaughter is allowed to enjoy her off-time any way she chooses?"

Sara knew Cade's comment hit home by the way her grandmother's eyes narrowed. She pinned the handsome cowboy with her severest glare.

"As long as you're not feeling neglected, Cade."

"Neglected?" His amused laugh turned many heads. "I run a ranch, Mrs. Woodward. There aren't enough hours in the day to keep on top of everything, let alone feel neglected."

"Perhaps you need a helper."

Sara's cheeks burned.

Why don't you just auction me off, Grandmother?

"I have quite a few helpers. My staff and I make a great team. But thanks for your concern." Cade smiled at her, then turned to Sara. "If you've got a minute, I'd like to talk about seating arrangements."

"Certainly. We can go over there, out of the way." She smiled kindly at Winnie who looked deflated. "You don't mind, do you, Grandma? After all, you said I should be available whenever the client wants to talk."

"It's a waste of wonderful music," Winnie grumbled, but when they sat down at a table, she hung around just long enough to thank Cade for her brooch while sneaking a peek at the seating chart he laid on the table. Then she abandoned them.

Sara leaned forward to study the paper. Her brows met in a frown of confusion.

"When did you learn how to make a seating chart?"

"Ha! Didn't know I could, did you? Never underestimate a rancher." Cade smoothed his hand over the wrinkled paper. When he glanced up his smile stretched all the way to his eyes. "Internet. I was a Boy Scout and I'm always prepared. Besides, I think the idea is usable. It should hold your grandmother back for a while anyway."

"Don't count on it. My mother saw your wink. She's busy putting two and two together as we speak. But thanks for trying." It was nice to have someone in her corner for a change. But Sara saw another emotion flicker across his face. Sadness?

"To be truthful, I enjoyed our little skirmish. Your grandmother reminds me quite a lot of my own. Emily was always playing what I called mind games, trying to psych you out so she could get you to do her will. Sometimes they didn't turn out very well."

"Oh?" He meant something specific.

"In my junior year my parents lived on the ranch, as well as my grandparents. A man and his daughter moved in next door. We were best friends." A smile flickered at the corner of Cade's mouth. "We were kindred souls, spent hours riding, racing and swimming. We competed on every level and yet we never argued."

"This wasn't Marnie?"

He burst out laughing.

"Hardly. Marnie was never into ranching. But Jayne was. She knew as much, or more, than I did. But my grandmother never accepted Jayne and as time went on, Jayne wanted less and less to do with me. The day after school finished, Jayne and her father suddenly left town. I later found out she was very sick. I also learned Emily had known all along and deliberately kept us apart because she thought it would be easier on me if I didn't get too close. I was furious."

Sara's heart welled with sympathy.

"It must have taken some time to heal the rift in your relationship."

"It did but only after I learned Jayne had fallen for someone else." He grimaced. "My grandmother tried to atone. I got over my anger but we lost too much time. Grandmother passed away not long after. My grandfather had a heart attack two months later."

"I'm sorry."

"So am I. The thing is, Sara, Emily did what she did out of love for me. Because she wanted the best for me. That doesn't erase her guilt, but it helps me understand. And forgive."

He was trying to help, but it didn't, not after the arguments Sara had to employ to get the time off she needed for the play. Her mother had made it sound as if she was refusing to do her duty, yet no one seemed to really need her here. Even Winnie looked back to normal, although she hadn't returned to the store since the day Cade had driven her home.

Take the big wedding last week—they'd all had some part in it, joked back and forth. Sara was the outsider, isolated, out of synch with their world. But she didn't want to talk about that now, so she focused on Karen's wedding. Then they discussed the play. She sketched her ideas for the various characters' masks hoping Cade would offer his perspective. She was beginning to value his ability to see things in a broader context.

"Because the play is about changing lemons into lemonade, we'll use a sequence of masks to illustrate the characters' adaptations to their problems," she explained. "A journey back to health."

"A journey. I like that. It's something the patients, even the young ones, will be able to identify with. I have a young friend, Lisa. I hope she'll be interested in trying out for a spot on the play. She was in an accident, and her scars are a barrier to the future she could have. I hope she'll consider it." He leaned back in his chair, his smile wide. "I wonder what your future will be like, Sara. Perhaps you'll be a famous name in five years. Is that what you want?"

"Fame?" She tried to imagine others applauding her work. "I don't know. I guess I haven't thought that far ahead."

His eyebrows lifted.

"All these years of dreaming and you haven't given any thought to what will happen when you finally achieve your goal?" He hunched forward, hands clasped on the tabletop. "I think it's important that you visualize what the end result will be to know if what you've sacrificed will be worth it."

"Sacrificed?" Her forehead pleated as she frowned.

"Yes."

She wanted to break free of her family's influence, but sacrifice?

"What makes you think I'm giving up something?"

Cade glanced over his shoulder to be sure no one was nearby, listening. Sara knew what he wanted to say was important.

"Nobody gets to have it all, Sara. When you go after one

thing, you naturally choose to opt out of others." His blue gaze glowed with his intensity. "So tell me, when you achieve your dream, when you're the top name in special effects, who is going to be there to watch you achieve it?"

"I don't know. That's a long way off."

"Not necessarily."

"Nice of you to say, but—" This was confusing. "Why is it important?"

"Don't you want the most important people in your world to be with you to celebrate when you finally make it?"

"I guess. Sure." She blinked, warned, "Katie's headed this way."

Cade's lips tightened, his frustration evident. "Is there somewhere we could go to talk? Somewhere private?"

"As I told you before, Woodwards has tons of rooms. Guess it's time for that tour. But—" Sara rose, frowning as she studied him "—won't disappearing make them more suspicious?"

"That's their problem. Lead the way."

Cade's fingers curled around her elbow as they moved through the room. There were plenty of birthday well-wishers mingling in the hall. Sara moved past them, led the way to the top floor and a tiny corner room with huge windows that overlooked the city.

They were alone.

"A tower room. Curious."

"I guess it's a relic from the original building. As a child, I played in here while my grandmother designed gowns in her office next door." Sara showed him the balcony. "I suppose nobody wanted this area because it's at the back of the building. But it became my hiding place."

He glanced around, then grinned at her.

"I can almost picture your hiding under that table, your big brown eyes peering out. This is the perfect place for an over-active imagination."

"Yes, it was. Why did you want to talk in private?"

"Because I'm concerned about you."

"Me?" she squeaked, unsure whether to laugh. "Why?"

"You've poured your heart and soul, your dreams, into achieving this goal of special effects. Am I right?"

She nodded.

"You would gain a lot. I'm sure the possibilities fill your mind. But look at this dream from a different perspective."

"Okay," she said warily.

"Close your eyes," he directed. When she'd done so, he continued. "Now, imagine you're in front of a huge audience. There are lights blazing on you. You're wearing a very elegant dress. It's your favorite shade of orange. Every eye is on you. An announcer states your name and the award you're receiving."

"I'm liking this dream," she mused.

"Good. Who do you see in the audience, clapping? Movie stars?"

"Maybe."

"Come on, Sara. Who do you see?"

"Coworkers, friends. People in the industry who understand what's involved to achieve that level of success." She opened her eyes, frustrated. "I don't know what you're getting at, Cade, so speak plainly."

"Did you envision your grandmother in the audience? How about Reese? Katie?"

"No. They don't like what I do. They want me to stay here, at Woodwards. I told you that." Why was he harping on this?

"You did tell me," he agreed. "You intimated you'd have to cut yourself off from them to achieve what you want. But don't you think that if you hit it big, they'd be there to cheer you on?"

"I—I don't know." She didn't get his concern. "Why does it matter so much?"

"I can't imagine you can look into your future and not expect them to be there with you. And I can't imagine you're okay with that."

"It's what I've had to learn," she said, irritated. "I have to do it on my own. Without my family."

"It's what you've chosen," he said quietly. "But it doesn't have to be like that. You have people who love and care for you very much, Sara. Maybe they don't show it the way you want, but you have to know your life would be much less rich without them. Make very sure you know what you're willing to give up to get that dream you're cherishing."

He studied her for several moments, then turned and walked to the door.

"Wait!" Surprised, she rose, followed him. "You're going?"

"The mare that gave birth is not doing well. I need to get home." His inscrutable face allowed no probing. He lifted one hand, cupped her chin in his palm. "Think about your future. Be careful what you wish for, Sara. You might just get it. And wish you hadn't."

Silence yawned between them. Sara could think of nothing to say to break it. A moment later Cade was gone and she was left to wonder why that undertone of pain threading his voice made her want to weep.

Chapter Six

Sara Woodward was a mess.

Friday afternoon, a week later, Cade leaned against the doorframe of his grandmother's painting house and stifled his urge to laugh out loud.

Sara's corkscrew wisps of hair refused to be confined to the knot bobbling up from the crown of her head. Faint streaks of gray-white clay decorated one cheek and the very tip of her chin. Her lips pinched together in a tight line, fingers nimbly working the clay, pushing and easing the medium until it resembled a face he recognized as a character in the hospital play.

And yet it wasn't a mirror image. The jut of the jawline, the pinch of the mouth, the flare of the eyes all held a winsomeness barely hinted at in the pair of masks already lying on the worktop. Amazed by her skill, Cade remained silent.

"I wish you were here to help me make them understand, Grandfather." Her whisper floated around the room. "Everyone's trying to change my mind, to convince me that this isn't what I want to do. Am I wrong to try?"

Sensing this wasn't a moment to intrude, Cade stepped

backward and left as quietly he could. At the bottom of the hill, a young girl waited with her mother in a car in front of his house, her face tight with strain.

"Lisa! I almost forgot you were coming for a lesson today." He opened her door, greeted her mother. "How was school?"

She made a face that required no translating. Cade recalled that Karen had worn that same look after certain days at the local comprehensive school.

"Forgot? Does that mean you're too busy?" She turned her face at an angle to hide the scars on her left cheek and neck, her voice trembling with diffidence.

Cade knew the uncaring attitude was a shield. Lisa wanted to learn to ride—badly. She just didn't want to admit it to him, in case she failed.

"Nope, not too busy. So don't think you can get out of it that easily." Cade bussed her nose with his fist. "I promised you six one-hour lessons in return for helping with the play and that's exactly what you'll get." He bent to speak to Lisa's mom. "Can I run her back home later? I've got some errands anyway."

"That would be great, Cade. Thanks. Bye, honey." They agreed on an approximate return time, then the car moved away, leaving a whirl of dust in its wake.

"Okay, Lisa. Ready to get started?"

Although a bit nervous, Lisa's connection with the mare he'd chosen was immediate. She was a natural horsewoman who needed little more than rudimentary directions. Graceful, intuitive and, most of all, willing to listen, Lisa was an apt pupil. Cade enjoyed his role as tutor. An hour later the teen looked tired but triumphant when they dismounted.

"You looked amazing. I wish I had your knack with animals." Sara sat on the top rail at the edge of the paddock, golden curls freely dancing in the breeze. "How long have you been riding?" she asked Lisa.

"Today's my first time."

"Really?" They chatted together for several moments while Cade stood silent, amazed by Sara's ability to get reserved, solemn Lisa to chatter.

"I didn't know he was your boyfriend." Lisa frowned at Sara, then glared at Cade as if he'd betrayed some secret.

"He's not my boyfriend."

Cade took silent exception to Sara's giggle which made it clear she found it impossible to cast him in that romantic role. He refused to dwell on why it stung.

"Cade's letting me use his grandmother's art studio to make some props for the play."

"Cool." Lisa's smile expanded. "Can I see?"

"I think you're supposed to brush your horse after you ride it, right?" Sara asked, looking to him for answers.

"It's called currying. And, yes, usually that's the rule. But this being Lisa's first time, I'll look after it." He undid the snap on her helmet. "Why don't you go check out Sara's work? I'll meet up with you both in a bit."

"Thanks, Cade. You're the best. That was an awesome ride." Lisa stood on tiptoe, kissed his cheek as she handed him the reins, then turned to Sara. "Let's go. I'm Lisa, by the way."

"I remember. You're playing the girl who has the accident." Sara's glance brushed over Lisa's damaged face as if she noticed nothing unusual. "You're great in that role."

Cade watched them leave with faint regret, wishing he'd thought of a good reason to be included. By the time he'd cared for the horses and washed up, an hour had passed and Lisa's mother had called with a change in plans. After reassuring her he would bring Lisa home eventually, Cade strode up the hill, anxious to see how the two females were faring.

Music, carried on a zephyr wind from the octagonal building, echoed across the valley. Cade nudged the open door and saw six masks lying in varying stages on the long table. Two bodies sat cross-legged on the floor, backs to the fireplace, heads bent over a sketchpad. He moved closer to hear the conversation.

"These are the masks I thought of for your character, Lisa. I thought they'd be perfect to show how you change. But if you don't like them then—"

"It's not that." The young girl stared at her hands, her embarrassment obvious. "I like them a lot, but—"

"Come on, tell me. I can't change anything if I don't understand." Sara nudged her with one shoulder, her voice very gentle. "What's wrong, Lisa?"

"It hurts."

"Hurts?" Sara's golden head reared back in surprise. "What do you mean?"

"When you brought some masks to practice the other day, I tried a couple on. They hurt. Here." Lisa lifted a hand to the side of her face, just in front of her ear, where her scar left a rippling reminder.

"Where the banding goes. I see." Sara chewed her bottom lip. "But we have to keep it on you somehow. Maybe if I made the fastening higher up?"

"That won't help." Lisa's head stayed bent. She refused to look at Sara.

"Why not?"

"It's worse higher up. The scar goes most of the way around." She parted her hair to expose the slash of red healing skin. "See what I mean?"

"Uh-huh. I get it."

"Maybe they should pick someone else."

"No, you're perfect for that role. We'll just have to think of another way."

But even though Cade waited, neither female came up with the solution that was so obvious to him. He hit the off button on the stereo. Gold and brunette heads twisted to stare at him.

"Oh, hi, Cade. Is it time to go now?" Lisa rose, brushed down her jeans. "Sorry, I wasn't watching the time."

"No problem." He moved in front of Sara, held out a hand to help her stand. "Why can't you use makeup on her?"

"I'm not—"

"She wouldn't have to wear a mask if you transformed her face with makeup," he interrupted, praying Sara would understand what he wasn't saying. He held on to her fingers a moment longer than necessary. "Isn't makeup what you do?"

"Yes, it is." Sara studied him for several minutes before she drew her hands away. She turned her focus on Lisa and grinned. "Why didn't we think of that?"

"Because I'm a genius," Cade suggested.

The ladies ignored him.

"But I wouldn't be like the other actors then." Lisa couldn't hide the tiny bit of hope threading through her voice. "They're all wearing masks."

"Doesn't matter." Sara began sketching. "Think of the audience. You're the main character. We're trying to show you changing. We could emphasize your scar for the first part of the story—"

"Emphasize it?" Lisa shrank away from Sara, her horrified gaze seeking Cade. "I don't want to emphasize it! I want to hide it so no one ever sees it."

"We'll do that, too, I promise." Sara set her sketchpad on a nearby table, her smile fading as she saw Lisa's disbelief. "You don't trust me."

Cade had put in hard work to get past Lisa's reticence, to get her to relate with him as a friend and not a nosy old neighbor. It had taken plenty of persuasion to get her to try out for the play. He prayed their relationship wasn't going to change, when she'd just begun to trust him.

"I can make your scar disappear, Lisa."

"Yeah, right." The young girl turned away, defeat dragging down her shoulders. "It was nice to meet you again. Can we go now?" she asked Cade, her eyes begging him to agree.

"I don't mean physically," Sara said softly. "But I can make it so that even a camera wouldn't notice."

"Sure you can." Lisa was shutting down.

"You won't let me prove it? Why? Are you too scared?"

Cade opened his mouth to ask Sara to back off. But the almost imperceptible shake of her blond head stopped him. Her gaze moved to Lisa and he followed it, somewhat surprised to see the teen's body language alter.

"I'm not afraid of anything." Her eyes flashed.

"I think you are. I think you're afraid that if you don't have that scar, you'll have nothing to hide behind. You won't have a good reason to stand on the sidelines, withdraw like you did at rehearsal." Sara touched one rigid shoulder as if to soften her words.

"So? It's just a stupid play. I went only because I promised Cade."

"Obviously he saw something in you that you can't see in yourself. He saw potential. But you have to do something with it." Sara wrapped one arm around the thin shoulders and hugged Lisa against her side. "You've got your whole life in front of you, sweetie. Boys, dating, love. Maybe marriage. There are so many things you can do. Don't you want to find out what your future could be?"

"I already know. What guy is going to want to date this?" Lisa drew her hair back to expose the cruel scar. "People stare. Boys avoid me."

Sara was doing her best, but it was time for Cade to help.

"People are curious about others. If you see something different about someone, don't you take a second look?" He smiled at her, softened his voice. "It's human nature. But when you let us get to know you, Lisa, we don't see any scar. You flash your pretty smile and all I see is a beautiful girl."

"You're not seventeen."

"You had to remind me?" Cade complained, glad she was at least listening. "I think you see the scar more than anyone else, kiddo, but if you feel it's such a barrier to building relationships, why won't you let Sara help?"

"She's not the first one who promised stuff like that." Lisa's soft mutter clearly expressed her doubts. "I've seen a ton of doctors, and I have drawers full of creams and potions. Not one of them ever did what they claimed."

"Because you want it gone. I'm not promising that, Lisa. But if you don't let me show you what I can do, you'll never know the difference it could make."

"You're probably selling some line of makeup."

"No, I'm not. You don't have to buy a thing. If you don't like what I do, we'll wash it off and no one will ever know."

"I don't know." Lisa chewed her bottom lip, her forehead pleated in a frown of doubt. "It sounds too good to be true."

Some women would have given up, but not Sara. Cade wanted to hug her.

"If nothing else, you'll get an inside view of a makeup artist's life and the tools we use. What do you say, Lisa?"

Cade held his breath.

"All right."

"We'll have to go to Woodwards. All my stuff is there."

"I'll drive both of you." He met their amused stares. "I want to see this transformation, too."

"You need a life, Cade," Lisa mocked.

"Oh, let him come. He's usually trying to avoid getting inside Woodwards." Sara tossed him a teasing grin. "He thinks it should be more manly."

"Cade was at Weddings by Woodwards?" Lisa blinked. "You're getting married?"

"He's planning his sister's wedding." Sara and the younger girl began strolling downhill toward the main house. "And doing a pretty good job of it, too."

Cade closed the studio doors, called Lisa's mom to ask permission then quickly followed the pair, catching snippets of their conversation. Sara explained about Karen's wedding, but when the subject changed, the wind snatched away their words. Judging by the looks he was getting though, they were talking about him. He picked up his pace.

"—too bad he isn't married," Lisa was saying. "He's great with kids. My brother goes to his boys' group. He loves it. Cade's like the father we wish we'd had. He doesn't expect kids to be angels. He lets them be who they are and he always answers our questions. Lots of adults put kids off when they ask stuff, you know. It's really annoying."

"He is rather unique."

Cade opened the front and back doors of his car, averting his eyes so he wouldn't get caught staring at Sara. Lisa climbed in the backseat, slamming the door behind her, but Sara paused next to him, her voice too soft to be overheard.

"You put yourself out there for a lot of people, Cade Porter. Why?"

He studied her tilted face, wondering what this tiny self-contained woman would say if he admitted he did whatever it took to stay busy, to stave off his loneliness, to ease the longing that never left the cracks in his heart.

"What's the point of life if you don't share it?" he finally managed.

"There you go again, answering a question with a question." A faint smile touched her mouth. "Just when I think I know you, I find out something I didn't expect. And it makes me wonder, who are you really, Cade?"

"An ordinary rancher who's simply trying to get two ladies into town so they can slap on the war paint and charm unsuspecting males."

"*Ordinary* is not a word that applies to you, Cade Porter." After a slight hesitation, Sara climbed inside. "Not even close."

The way she said it eased his trepidation about reentering the fussy bridal store.

"I could have driven." Sara kept watching him.

"But then you would have had to drive Lisa back. This way I get to enjoy both your company a little longer," he shot back, delighted by the prospect.

"And if the family is there?" Sara's knowing smile mocked him.

Uh-oh. He'd forgotten about the Woodward family.

"I'll deal with it."

"Sure you will, tough guy." Tossing him a mocking smile, Sara turned her attention to Lisa, quizzing her about her taste in fashion, hair and a host of other female things Cade vaguely remembered his sister discussing.

By the time they arrived, the two were giggling merrily as they sang along with a tune playing on his radio.

"Wow! Looks busy today. Go around back, Cade," Sara directed. "You can use my parking spot."

He obeyed, swallowed hard when she pointed out her parents' and siblings' cars.

"At least Grandmother isn't here." She chuckled. "I don't think. Come on, you two. Maybe we can sneak in without anyone noticing."

"Yeah, sure." Cade winced as the door opened and Mrs. Woodward pounced.

"Cade! How lovely to see you again." Sara's mother hugged him like a long-lost relative. Katie appeared, handed him one of the twins and dumped the other into Sara's arms.

"You're answers to my prayers. Reese is closeted with the Sutcliffes, explaining their bill in copious detail. I've got a reception going in the crystal room. Be a doll and keep these two busy, will you? Hello," she said to Lisa before disappearing.

"Mom, I—"

"Sorry, dear. I'm working with a new client. Just came for a sample." She waved a tiny bit of white satin at them. "Cade, I hope you'll stay around. We haven't chatted in ages."

Hardly ages. Two days. Fiona had chatted *at him* two days ago.

"Sorry," he apologized. "I have to take Lisa home when Sara's finished. Maybe another time."

"Yes, maybe." Sara's mother smiled at Lisa before fluttering away.

"Horsie?"

"No horsie, Brady. Come on, let's get into a room before someone gives us something else to do." Sara led the way, but once they'd gathered in what was clearly a bride's dressing room, she stopped and frowned at the twin she was holding. "How are we going to get anything done now?"

"We three men will go for ice cream while you ladies beautify." The idea emerged full blown, and Cade was grateful. The tiny silk sofas wouldn't support him for ten minutes, never mind the kids. "Do they have a stroller or something?"

Sara fetched it, helped him install the twins before she squatted down and read them the riot act face-to-face.

"If you two are naughty, Mr. Porter's going to bring you right back and you won't get a bit of ice cream. Got it?"

The two heads nodded.

"We're good, Auntie Sara. We like ice cream."

"I know you do." She kissed their heads, then showed Cade where she'd stored a pack of wet wipes. "You are going to need these, so keep them handy. Are you sure you're up to the twins? Both—at one time? Alone?"

If they'd been quintuplets, he'd have accepted the challenge just to get out of the cloying feminine room and the possibility that Sara's father would show up and invite himself along. He'd only met Thomas Woodward a couple of days ago, but the dark eyes, so like Sara's, and the intense way they seemed to bore into his thoughts, scared Cade.

And he wasn't ready to analyze why.

"Cade? What's wrong with you? Are you sick?" Sara jiggled his arm, her face peering into his.

"I'm fine. I'm sure I can handle the twins." Cade stepped backward, found himself enmeshed in a beehive of ribbon he'd knocked over. "Sorry." He waited while Sara patiently worked to release him. At last he gained the doorway. "How long do you need?"

"Is half an hour asking too much?"

"A breeze for someone with my copious capabilities. As someone recently told someone else, I'm not just an ordinary rancher." He grinned at her rolling eyes, waved at Lisa. "Don't be scared. Have fun."

"This might help you escape quietly, super rancher." Sara handed each twin a candy sucker, then smiled in that generous way that lit up her whole face. She touched his hand. "Thank you, Cade. Now go."

He didn't argue. He stepped out of the room and headed for the main door. And he almost made it. Except for a tiny woman who popped out of the display window door and stepped squarely in front of him.

"Dear boy. How nice of you to stop by to see our Sara. She's a lovely girl, and I know she simply adores you. Why, she spends almost every waking moment planning how she can get to your ranch." Winifred Woodward's smile hid none of her thoughts. "The two of you make a lovely couple."

Cade grabbed four pudgy fingers just in time.

"Excuse me, Mrs. Woodward, but the boys are very sticky. I wouldn't want your creations ruined." He adroitly worked the stroller past her and through the main door, grateful when an incoming customer held it open.

"Isn't he handsome with the twins? Cade is such a delight to our Sara—" Winifred's chirping voice sped him on.

"Um, bye now." Cade didn't slow his steps until they'd gone two blocks and it was clear no one was following him. "Okay, guys. Let's go find some ice cream."

"Horsie?"

"Not today, Brady." Cade tipped his face into the sun and let it soak through his skin, soothe his heart.

How wonderful to be able to take your children for ice cream. Did Reese do that often? Did his heart pinch tight when he tucked these precious ones into their bed every night? Did he agonize over choices he'd made for them the way Cade had agonized about Karen?

"Walk." Brady angled one leg over the side.

"Not just now, okay? First we find ice cream."

"'Kay."

The twins didn't so much eat the ice cream as smear it all over everything. But it seemed funny to Cade. In fact, everything was, and he couldn't stop grinning. Once they'd finished, he'd cleaned them off. Then he took the long way back, anxious to allow Sara as much time as possible to work with Lisa. He had a hunch that both of them needed the other.

By the time he pushed the stroller through Woodwards' grand entrance, the twins were fast asleep. A Woodwards' attendant he'd seen before took a moment from her discussion with a client to wave at him and motion toward the back.

Cade pushed the stroller down the hall, trying to remember which of the many white doors he'd been in earlier. Voices drew him and he stepped eagerly forward. The conversation stopped him in his tracks.

"She's happier here and you know it, Thomas."

"I don't know that, Fiona. Our daughter has never been an open book to me. Being her father doesn't give me automatic insight into her mind. But if Reese thinks she's found a kindred soul in this Cade fellow, I'm inclined to go with our son's instincts."

"She's pouring a lot of effort into this play she's working on with him." Reese sounded amused. "I've found sketches all over the place."

"As a way to get them together, it was fine. But I'm concerned that now she's working with this girl on makeup. The original plan was to get her back into the business," Winifred said, her voice firmer than he'd ever heard it. "Our business. The wedding business. That's where Cade Porter comes in. He's perfect for her."

"They do look lovely together," Katie murmured.

"It's clear Sara is smitten. It's Cade this and Cade that. I've never seen her so animated. I'm glad we got her back," Fiona said. "Sara belongs here."

Got her back? Cade's temper surged.

Time to put an end to this.

"Excuse me for interrupting." Mindful of the sleeping boys, Cade stepped into the room and eased the stroller to a quiet corner. "I couldn't help overhearing what you were saying."

Anger threatened to sidetrack him, but Cade focused. He had to make them understand while protecting Sara's privacy.

"I know that you all love Sara, that you've worried over her while she's been away and that you'd prefer to have her remain in Denver, to be a part of your business. Believe me, having my sister overseas allows me to empathize with your desire to keep your family together. But you cannot use me to do it."

"We weren't—"

Cade pinned the matriarch with his sternest glare. Winifred had the grace to blush.

"I like Sara very much." Satisfaction wreathed five faces. Cade pushed on. "She's been great with my sister's wedding and with the play, both of which are very dear to me. We've built a friendship. But that's all there is. That's all there can be."

"May I ask why? You two seem quite close." Katie leaned forward, intent on finding answers to the questions evident in the others' eyes. "You're always calling each other, sharing lunch, not to mention those evening get-togethers."

"None of which is personal. We have the wedding and the play in common, but that's all. So it would be best if you put an end to your matchmaking right now." He pulled himself to his full height and forced the words from his lips. "There is no point in hoping we'll become a couple because it won't happen. I won't let it happen."

Now he'd shocked them. Good. It was time to end a few fantasies.

"You may believe I'll change my mind if you can just throw us together enough." He saw hope dawn and hurried to squelch it. "I assure you, that is not going to happen. Sara is a fine woman whom any man would be proud to love, but I will never be that man."

Disbelief filled their eyes, but Cade knew that if he didn't shut them down, they'd go on scheming for a way to circumvent his decision. He pressed on.

"Listen to me. I was engaged once. And my fiancée died right before our wedding. I spent a long time seeking God about that, asking Him to show me His will for my future. He did." He kept his voice steely firm. "God does not intend for me to marry. His choice for my life lies in a different direction."

"But—"

He shook his head at Winifred.

"No buts. Nothing you do or say or try will reverse my decision to obey God. This issue is settled, and I will not change my mind." The defeat filling their faces made him pause, but it was better to be honest. He cleared his throat, struggled to soften what had to be said.

One of the twins stirred, so Cade lowered his voice.

"I'm telling you this not because I have any desire to share my private life, but because I am concerned that you don't realize how your actions are undermining Sara. You're her family. Of course she loves you and wants to please you. But even though she's your daughter, sister, granddaughter, she is also a talented creator. She is driven by a strong desire to pursue her skills, to attain a dream she's cherished for years, a dream she believes only her grandfather would understand."

"Makeup is a waste of her talents," Winifred snapped.

"A waste? Because it doesn't fit in with *your* plans?" He touched the old woman's shoulder. "Have you seen what she can do? In a way, Sara's work brings people their dreams every bit as much as yours does. Her work offers people a different perspective on life. Her work is insightful, it's refreshing, but most of all, it is *her* choice."

Winifred looked ready to interrupt. Cade pressed on.

"Sara doesn't ask you to share it or even approve of her work. She's strong and determined and she will succeed. All she hopes is that her family will support her." He spoke directly to Winifred. "By trying to force her to do something else, you are fracturing the very relationship you say you want to maintain. That hurts Sara, because she loves you."

"We all love her."

"If you love someone, you love who and what they are. You don't try to change them to make them into what you want them to be."

"That's unfair." Her father bristled to his feet.

"If so, I apologize. I'll go now." Cade checked to be certain the boys were still asleep and turned away. But at the last minute he couldn't leave without one more plea. He turned, begged them, "Please stop trying to manipulate her. And me. It hurts Sara and I can't believe that's what you want to do."

He left the room but jerked to a halt outside.

Sara stood there, her cheeks tearstained. She dredged up a watery smile.

"We both know it won't help, but thank you for trying."

"You're welcome." Cade tamped down the urge to wrap his arms around her and tell her just how lovable she was. Instead he smoothed away a ringlet entangled in her eyelashes. "Where's Lisa? I want to see what she looks like."

Wordlessly, Sara led him to another door, pushed it open.

"Hi, Cade." Lisa, confident, vibrant and very beautiful, grinned at him. "Do you like it?" she asked, twirling around to give him a 360-degree view.

"You look—fantastic." It was the truth. Her big gray eyes sparkled at him, emphasizing her smile, a natural one, not forced. Her hair curved around her face, enhancing her beauty instead of hiding it. "Your hair is different."

"Did you know Woodwards has a stylist in the building, just in case someone needs help?" Lisa wrapped her arms around her waist and checked her reflection in the mirror, as if she couldn't quite believe what she saw. "She took a few snips here and there and this happened. This is the best day of my life."

"No, it's the first," Sara assured her. "Your life is all ahead of you. Don't forget that. And don't let anything steal your joy in it."

Anything or anyone? Cade wondered.

"Sara showed me how to do the makeup. I can do it at home." Lisa launched into an explanation of the steps Sara had shown her to disguise the scar.

"You can do it anywhere. Just remember to cleanse really well, Lisa. Your scar is still healing." Sara patted the girl's shoulder like a proud mother.

"You're not even looking at me, Cade," Lisa complained. "Do you see something I missed?" She twisted from one side to the other, looking for problems.

Cade cursed his stupidity, but Sara had the matter well in tow.

"Hey, what did I tell you, Lisa?"

"If you act confident, most people will assume you are."

"And?" Sara grinned at her, egging her into something.

Cade just didn't know what.

"I was wondering if we could go for a soda before you take me home," Lisa asked him.

"At Pelligrino's," Sara added.

That name—wait a minute, wasn't that the place Lisa had wept about last week. Something about being excluded? Cade glanced at Sara, caught her imperceptible nod.

"Why not?" he agreed. "I deserve a treat with two lovely ladies."

"You just had ice cream." Sara hooked her arm through both his and Lisa's and led them out of the room. "Didn't you?"

Cade heard her family scurry into the hall behind but he ignored them.

"I didn't actually eat the ice cream," he explained. "Mostly I wore it. And cleaned it up."

"That's my nephews." Sara winked at Lisa. "Poor baby. He deserves a triple thick chocolate shake, don't you think?"

"Definitely. With extra syrup and whipped cream."

"I'll settle for black coffee," Cade mumbled, trying not to shudder.

"Boring."

Sara teased him nonstop for the rest of the afternoon and all the way back to the ranch, after they'd dropped a giggling Lisa at her front door.

"That went well, don't you think?" She climbed out of the car before he could help.

"I think you're far more talented than I ever imagined," he said, leaning against the hood as he watched her pet his dog. "And I imagined a lot of talent."

"It didn't take talent to see Lisa was miserable or to encourage her self-confidence. She's a lovely girl."

"So are you. Thank you for taking time for her."

"Oh, don't thank me, Cade. It was such fun to see her eyes light up, to hear her laugh when those girls came over in the coffee shop." Sara straightened, smiled at him, her eyes dreamy. "That's the best thanks anyone could have, that and knowing she'll dive back into her life."

Cade glanced at the big house he'd grown up in and knew he didn't want to go back inside, alone. He studied Sara, her blond hair loosened by the wind which also snagged at her sweater. She pulled her keys out of her jeans pocket.

Sara was going to leave, to get in her car and go back to her big family.

He wanted her to stay.

"How about a riding lesson?"

Sara had been staring at the mountains, her eyes faraway. She turned slightly, studied him with open curiosity.

"Hasn't your day been disrupted enough?"

"Nope." He shoved his hands in his pockets, hoping, praying she'd stay. "Well?"

"It will be dark soon."

"We can use the riding barn. Plenty of light."

Cade thought she was going to refuse. But suddenly that wide, generous smile flashed and she nodded, brown eyes darkening with what he hoped was anticipation.

"Okay. But you may be sorry."

Deep in the recesses of his soul, Cade knew he wouldn't be sorry. And that worried him.

He'd assured her parents he and Sara were just friends. He needed to remind himself of that.

Again.

Chapter Seven

"You should have asked me to ride earlier." Sara grabbed the horn of the saddle, struggling to stay on the horse's back.

"Why?" Cade leaned over and snatched the rein she'd lost.

"I could have upped my insurance first." She loved the way he laughed, deep and rich, without restraint. "I hurt in places I didn't know existed. Much as you're enjoying my pain, I have to get off or I won't be walking tomorrow."

"It's not that bad." He swung off his horse, led hers to the dismount stand and helped, actually caught her as she half tumbled from the horse. "Is it?"

"Yes."

"Uh-oh."

His concern touched a sensitive spot in her heart that hadn't existed before. At least Sara didn't think it had.

"You'd better hit the hot tub."

The mere thought of jets of water rushing over her sore muscles made her groan.

"Don't even joke about it."

"What joke? I have a hot tub. Why shouldn't you use it?"

Oh, so many reasons came to mind. Like, she was tired and

her mouth said things before her brain made sure they were appropriate. Or that she was beginning to depend on Cade Porter way too much. Or that she didn't want this day to end.

First he'd had that chat with her family, warning them off their matchmaking. Then he'd insisted on riding lessons even after she'd explained how much her parents had spent on riding lessons for her—to no avail. If only she'd known then what she knew now about how wonderful it was to be around a cowboy.

"Sara?" His hand touched her arm, drawing her back to reality.

"Sorry. Daydreaming." She studied his serious face and smiled. "I'm fine. Really. Or I will be."

"I'm serious about the hot tub. There are tons of suits. Karen always had someone over. You could soak out the kinks while I shower. Then I'll warm up whatever Mrs. Brown has left for dinner. What do you say?"

She wanted to say yes.

The family's incessant questions about the play made mealtimes little more than interrogations. What could it hurt to escape, if only for a little while?

"Only if you're positive I'm not making more work for you. I know running this place isn't the piece of cake you pretend it is."

"Not a piece of cake, but most things go fairly smoothly. I can take a few hours off here and there and not lose the ranch."

Cade showed her how to care for her horse. Once their mounts were fed and watered, they walked to the house. Sara struggled to keep up, muscles protesting as she climbed the stairs and stepped through the front door.

"There's a closet back here," he told her, striding through the kitchen to pull open a big white door. At least a dozen swimsuits hung inside. "Take your choice. You can change in the bathroom here. The towels are on the bottom shelf. Slip on a pair of slippers. The ground is cold."

"Thank you."

"I'll open the lid and turn on the jets. Get in whenever you're ready. I'm going to have a shower. Okay?" He waited until she nodded, then opened the back door and left.

Sara shivered as the cool air rushed in. It felt like snow would cover the mountaintops tonight. She selected a one-piece suit of bright red. It fit perfectly. With a huge bath sheet wrapped around her like a sarong, she slid on a pair of the rubber slippers he'd indicated and stepped out of the bathroom.

Cade wasn't on the deck where the tub steamed into the cool night. Moving quickly, Sara shed her shoes and towel and lowered herself into the warm water. For a few moments it felt very hot, but her body adjusted quickly and she soon found a perfect spot to recline where the bubbles massaged her back and feet.

The deck was part of a yard space that perched above a wooded area. When the jets shut off, sounds of a bubbling brook carried to her. There was no bright lighting here. Instead the world lay bathed in intermittent moonlight and the faint glow of dim landscape lights.

Sara closed her eyes and listened. At first the night seemed silent. But as she relaxed she caught the whinny of a horse, the rustle of leaves and the slither of small animals through the underbrush.

Cade was so lucky. He could come out here every night and no one would demand to know how he'd spent his day. He'd have no one questioning his decisions, no one pushing him to change his mind, to do something he didn't want to. Here he was free to be and do exactly what he wanted.

"You haven't fallen asleep, have you?"

The quiet rumble of his voice didn't jar the evening stillness but rather meshed into it. Sara shook her head before realizing he might not see her.

"No. Just relaxing. You have a beautiful view here. I can hear the wind dancing with the leaves."

He asked her if she wanted the jets back on.

"No, thanks. We can talk better if they're off."

He handed her a big steaming mug of coffee. Drawing a chair nearby, he sat down, tilted his face to the sky, fingers cupped around his own cup. Sara tasted and found he'd made it exactly the way she loved.

"I come out here quite a bit at night," he said, a tiny rasp edging his quiet voice. "To think. And to pray. It always feels like I'm a little closer to God when I'm alone out here, in the world He created."

Because she never felt very close to God anywhere, Sara remained silent.

"It's easier to talk to Him out here. Easier to hear His answers, too, without all the noise of life swirling around you."

"What do you talk about?" The question slipped out without thought. Sara held her breath, hoping his answer would help with her own doubts.

"Everything. Anything." He shrugged. "When Karen first went overseas, I came out here a lot. Easier to admit my fears in the dark I guess."

"I'm sure it's natural to have fears when she's in such a dangerous situation."

"Natural that they come maybe, but wrong to let them hang around. The Bible tells us not to worry about anything. God knows the situations and what will happen. He loves Karen even more than I do. I have to trust that He will do His very best for her because of that love."

"So what do you talk about?"

"Everything." He turned his head to study her, his eyes showing his puzzlement. "Don't you pray, Sara?"

"Not anymore."

"Why not?"

She thought about it for a minute.

"I guess because I never felt I got an answer. Praying always sounds like a big want list anyway," she said, defending herself.

"It shouldn't be."

"Why not?"

"Because praying is about a relationship, one that's ongoing."

Once she'd had an intense longing to experience just such a relationship. Tonight Cade's words stirred it up again, longings she'd thought she'd buried. Sara fiddled with the water as she strove for nonchalance.

"Aren't we supposed to ask for what we want?"

"Yes, but prayer isn't only about asking, Sara. Continually asking for stuff isn't the way we converse with other humans and it shouldn't be how we pray. Prayer is talking to God. We talk about what happened today, about what we wish would happen, about our hopes and our dreams. We ask questions and we wait for answers."

"But God doesn't speak."

Cade smiled. "Sure He does, Sara."

She blinked. "How?"

"All kinds of ways."

"Well, I haven't heard Him."

"Are you sure?" He didn't laugh at her or mock her, for which she was grateful. "Did you ever memorize Scripture verses?"

"When I was a kid. I've forgotten most of them."

"That's too bad. Because Scripture is God talking to us.

When we memorize it, it's there in our minds and God reminds us of what He's said."

She thought of her grandmother's favorite verse.

All things work together for good for those who love God.

"A minute ago I compared prayer to a human relationship," Cade said, tilting back to study the night sky, "but it goes way beyond that. God is our Father, but He's also God of the universe. He's holy and worthy of honor and respect. When we talk to Him, we must also take time to be quiet and listen for what He has to say."

"But I never hear anything!" The words burst out of her in a rush of pent-up frustration. "That's partly why I gave up."

"Lots of people have the same problem, Sara. They blame God for not paying attention, but that's not the problem."

"So what is?"

Her eyes had adjusted to the dark, so she saw a half smile tug the corners of Cade's mouth.

"God, our God, who made the universe out of nothing, isn't going to come running just because His spoiled children demand His presence right here, right now. He wants us to spend time with Him, to try to understand His nature. You can't do that in thirty-second bursts. You need to make time every day to talk to Him, to let Him speak through the Bible to you. You have to be silent, to listen attentively if you want to hear His voice."

Cade continued, explaining how God fit into his everyday world. She'd heard it all before, of course, but Cade made his relationship seem so natural, genuine. Finally Sara admitted the truth to herself. She wanted what he had—that solid, heart-deep knowledge that God loved you exactly as you were and that He was on your side. That you weren't alone.

What she wasn't sure of was whether she could get it.

"I'm babbling on and you're probably roasting in there. I'll check on our meal while you get out and change. Don't bother about closing the tub. I'll do it. You need to get inside before you get a chill."

Sara held his gaze with her own.

"Yes, Grandmother," she said, keeping her voice meekly obedient.

He hooted with laughter.

"Sorry. I guess I fell back into my Karen's-big-brother mode for a minute. See you inside—whenever you're ready."

As she climbed out of the tub and swathed the towel around her rapidly chilling skin, Sara realized she didn't want Cade to think of her as his little sister.

But all through their delicious meal, during the long laughter-filled board game they played and even during the solitary ride home, she couldn't quite decide how she did want Cade to think of her.

Friend?

Yes.

But more than that?

That made her nervous.

Maybe she'd try talking to God about it.

"Your mother said you'd been sitting out here for ages. What are you doing, darling?"

"Hi, Grandmother."

Because Winnie wore a thick coat, fuzzy gloves and had a wool scarf wrapped around her neck, Sara scooted over, patted the edge of the lounge chair for her to sit down. She tucked half of the wool blanket she'd been using around her grandmother's knees, hoping no one else would come to find them for at least a few minutes. She needed to talk to someone or she would explode with questions.

"I'm meditating."

"On what, dear?"

"God." It had taken more than a week to build up enough courage to ask, but now that she had, Sara tossed caution aside. "Why doesn't He hear me, Granny?"

"He does. Always. Every word."

"Then why doesn't He answer?" Sara pulled the small Bible from her pocket. "Someone told me to read the Bible and then wait for God to talk to me. I've been reading and waiting all week and I haven't heard an answer to my question."

"Maybe you're asking the wrong question." Winnie's gloved fingers brushed her cheek. "Darling, you grew up knowing about God, about His ways. Surely—"

"But that's just it! I knew about Him. I didn't know Him. I still don't." Frustration sent a rush of tears to her eyes. "I feel like I've never really known God. I blindly accepted what I was told, but it's not enough now."

"I don't suppose it could be. Christianity is a personal issue."

"Yes. So if I'm to really trust God, I need to experience who and what He is for myself. It's not enough to have other people tell me."

"That's the best thing you can say, darling. It's from needing to know that we really begin to seek God. The Bible says that when we seek Him, we will find Him. It's a promise, Sara. Here, let me show you." Winnie flicked through the Bible to Psalms. "Read this."

"'The Lord is fair in everything He does and full of kindness. He is close to all who call on Him sincerely. He fulfills the desires of those who reverence and trust Him; He hears their cries for help and rescues them. He protects all those who love Him.'"

The words pinged into her brain.

"It doesn't say God is close to us when we feel Him, Sara.

It says He is close to us when we call on Him. Period. No question. See this verse? 'His joy is in those who reverence him, those who expect Him to be loving and kind.'"

"Expect?"

"Of course." Winnie's fingers brushed across her cheek. "God wants you to expect His goodness. He loves it when we recognize that He is always at work for our benefit."

"Whether or not I sense it."

"Yes." Winnie inhaled. "Do you sense oxygen? Do you wake up every morning and wonder if there will be oxygen in the air? Of course not. You've accepted that the earth's atmosphere holds oxygen which humans breathe and you expect it to be there. It's the same with God. If you've accepted Him into your life, He is there, whether or not you are always aware of it."

"But—"

Winnie wrapped an arm around her shoulder and hugged her close.

"God doesn't have degrees of knowing, Sara. He leaves the relationship up to us. If we want to know Him, we can, but how much or how well is entirely our decision. God does not force himself on us."

"You're saying that if I don't feel connected to God, it's my fault?"

"Yes, darling, I am. There's a verse in Romans." She flicked through the Bible, pointed. "Here it is. Read this, Sara. Out loud."

"'Who then can ever keep Christ's love from us? When we have trouble or calamity, when we are hunted down or destroyed, is it because He doesn't love us anymore? And if we are hungry or penniless, or in danger, or threatened with death, has God deserted us?'" Sara glanced at her grandmother. "Why are you smiling, Granny?"

"You're not the first one to ask these questions, Sara. I've had my doubts, too. I think everyone does. But God knows our hearts. Go to verse thirty-eight."

"'For I am convinced that nothing can ever separate us from His love. Death can't, and life can't. The angels won't and all the powers of hell itself cannot keep God's love away. Our fears for today, our worries about tomorrow, or where we are—high above the sky, or in the deepest ocean—nothing will ever be able to separate us from the love of God.'"

Sara fell silent, stunned by the clarity of those verses. How could she have missed them? All those years of wondering— why hadn't she noticed before?

"You see, dear, regardless of what we feel, God's love is there. Always."

Winnie didn't state the obvious, that Sara might have heard those words if she'd gone to church with the rest of the family this morning or anytime in the last two years.

"Thank you, Grandmother."

"We should talk more often. Especially about God. I've been remiss there." Winifred pushed the blanket off her knees and rose. "I'm going inside before I get chilled. Why don't you come, too? You shouldn't sit out here alone."

"I like it. Besides, I'm not cold. In fact, the sun feels really warm this afternoon." Sara wouldn't admit how much she'd needed to escape the family's questions about Cade and the wedding and the play. "But you go in. You shouldn't have stayed out, not when you've been so sick."

"Oh, pooh! I'm old, not dying. A little case of the sniffles doesn't mean I'm going to quit living. I have too much to do." The words lost their emphasis when Winnie began coughing.

"I thought I heard you." Sara's father stepped onto the patio, beckoned. "Come on, Mother. Inside." He gave Sara a stern look. "She shouldn't be out here."

"Leave the girl alone, Thomas. We needed to talk. Now I need a hot, sweet cup of tea. Lead the way." Winnie tossed a wink at Sara, then grasped her son's arm and let him usher her inside, complaining about his bossiness as she went.

The pool deck fell silent again, except for the birds pecking the few ash berries still clinging to a tree. Sara studied the familiar landscape.

God was here. She could hardly imagine it.

"I want to get to know You," she whispered, feeling her way through the prayer. "I want to believe that I'm not alone, that You are there all the time. Please, help me?"

She sat there for a long time. Sometimes she read the words in her Bible, sometimes she whispered a prayer, sometimes she simply waited and listened. When a hand gripped her shoulder, she had no idea how much time had passed, only that the entire patio was in the shade and she was no longer alone.

"Cade!" She stared into his handsome face, half bemused. "What are you doing here?"

"You missed practice. Olivia called me. She wondered if something was wrong."

"I forgot." Sara studied him, noted the tiny fan of lines around the edges of his eyes, the way they intensified when he smiled. "I'm sorry you were disturbed."

"I wasn't disturbed. I like to see the progress. Today Olivia kept them busy running through their lines." He lifted his hand away from her shoulder and suddenly the world felt chilly. "Are you all right, Sara? Your mother let me in as they were leaving. She said you'd been out here alone all afternoon."

"It was warm and sunny earlier and I needed some quiet time." She shivered as the coolness penetrated to her consciousness. "Did you miss your dinner because of me?"

"Sort of." Cade grinned, eyes dancing with some hidden message. "Mrs. Brown doesn't come on Sundays so I fend for myself."

"Meaning?" Sara led the way inside the house, shed her jacket.

"Scrambled eggs for breakfast. Canned soup for lunch. That's the extent of my cooking ability. I usually go out for dinner." He shook his head when she reached out for his jacket. "Wanna come with me?"

"You're all dressed up," she said, only then noticing his black suit and crisp white shirt. "What's the occasion?"

"Aimée's birthday. I told you about it last week, remember?"

Sara didn't.

"So, will you come?"

"I don't have a gift," she said, wishing she'd remembered. A night out, with laughter, fun—she could have used that.

"I do. A gift certificate." He pulled a card from his pocket, showed her the note from Denver's hottest women's boutique. "Aimée loves shopping there."

"I see."

"It's from both of us. Come on." Cade's smile embraced his entire face. "Surely you're not going to turn down a meal at Cartier's?"

Sara considered her choices. Brood here at home, alone, or go to a birthday party with an attractive man. Some decision.

"Have I got time to change?"

Cade checked his watch.

"About ten minutes. Tops."

"I'll be ready." Sara raced toward the stairs.

"Yeah. Sure you will." His laughter chased her up to her room.

He wasn't laughing when she came down. In fact, Cade seemed oddly silent as they rode toward the restaurant.

"You'd better tell me what's wrong before we go in," she said when he pulled into a parking place. "Is the dress wrong? Do I have spinach in my teeth? Am I missing one earring?" She reached a hand up to her earlobe to check.

"No, to all of the above."

"Then what's wrong?"

"Why do you think something is wrong?" Cade fiddled with his key ring, only glancing at her after a prolonged silence that made Sara shift uncomfortably on the seat. "Nothing is wrong. As I've already told you, you look lovely."

"But my dress—is the orange too L.A.? Why didn't you say so? I don't want to stick out— What?" she demanded crankily when his finger dropped to rest on her lips.

"You're a beautiful woman, Sara. This dress, in your signature color, makes your beauty even more obvious. You look exactly right. Perfect for Aimée's party."

"You're sure?" If it wasn't the way she looked, then what was it?

"I'm sure. Let's go inside."

Sara waited until he opened her door, accepted his hand of help as she alighted. She kept her fingers tucked into his arm as they walked into the restaurant filled with happy laughter. Cade *seemed* perfectly normal. He greeted their hosts with a handshake and a hug, added his gift to the stack in front of a massive birthday cake and introduced Sara to a host of people.

But despite the pretense, Sara knew something wasn't right. After the meal, she excused herself and took cover in the ladies' room where she squeezed her eyes closed and whispered a prayer for help, using her newfound faith.

"I don't know what's wrong, God. Can You please be with me, help me to do the right thing tonight?"

Not much as prayers went, but as she emerged from the

room, Sara knew God had heard. Her spirit soared—until she saw Cade talking to Leon, who had just given her the oddest look.

Surely they weren't arguing at Aimée's party!

Chapter Eight

"Let it go, Leon. Sara was at home, alone. I brought her to celebrate Aimée's birthday. That's all there is to it."

"But why Sara? That is what I ask. You brought Olivia Hastings to dinner four months ago. I understood you were being kind to her because she was a newcomer to our church. That was nice."

"I'm a nice guy."

"And I am serious." Leon's glare cut to the heart of the matter. "Sara Woodward does not need kindness. There must be a dozen men in this room alone who know her and would be pleased to talk to her, but you scare them away with your fierce face. You do not look at her as you looked at Ms. Hastings, my friend. So?"

"We're friends, but that's all. And you know why, Leon."

"I know you say it's because you believe God has decreed you are to remain single." Leon made a face.

"Not that difficult a conclusion when you consider my history."

"Your history doesn't have to be your future," Leon complained. "I understand you want to obey God, but are you absolutely certain about His will? I thought I knew He didn't want us to have children, but lately we've been praying and thinking about foster children as a way to reach out and share our love. I feel God is leading us in that direction."

"Really?" Cade grinned. "Great."

"Yes, but what I'm saying is that I don't think I understood God correctly. I think I put my own interpretation on what happened because I didn't want Aimée to hurt anymore." Leon frowned. "Perhaps you've done the same, confused your own feelings with—"

He left the words hanging when Cade touched his arm.

"I'm sure I understand God, Leon. Marriage isn't for me. Anyway, Sara isn't interested in a relationship. She isn't even staying in Denver. She has a career to return to. We're friends, but that is all we can be."

"I think you're not totally truthful with yourself, my friend. Times like this I wish your sister was home. Karen was always the most sensible of you two. She would tell you that when you look at Sara Woodward, you aren't seeing her as simply a friend." Leon lifted an eyebrow. "If you were honest, you would admit it."

"Quiet, Leon." Cade shook his head when he noticed Sara walking toward them. "No more of this. Or I'll make an excuse to leave."

"And Aimée will get on my case, huh?" Leon sighed but dredged up a smile when Sara joined them. "I'm so glad you could be here, my dear. Now if you can coax Cade out of his bad mood, I'll owe you big-time." After a meaningful glance at Cade, Leon hurried away.

Sara frowned.

"Why are you in a bad mood?"

"I'm not." Why hadn't he stayed home tonight?

"But Leon said—"

"Leon's bugging me. Forget it. Would you like some punch?" He led her toward the three-tiered punch bowl that drizzled a pink frothy concoction from each level.

"What's in it?" Sara asked, bending to study the changing lights inside the tower.

"Cranberries and something. Leon has a cranberry fetish." He handed her a small glass, watched her nose wrinkle when she tasted it and laughed. "Coffee it is."

"It's not that it isn't good," she assured him. "It's more that I prefer my cranberries with my turkey."

"You and me both." He went to find the coffee urn. When he came back, Sara was still standing where he'd left her.

"This must be the punch fountain Karen describes in her album." Sara walked around the table twice, inspecting it thoroughly. "Some clear fizzy soda would really make it bubble. Which would make it fitting for a New Year's Eve wedding, don't you think?"

"Do you ever stop thinking about weddings?" he asked, then wished he'd kept silent when her eyes flared with surprise and something else. Hurt? "I'm sorry."

"What's wrong, Cade?"

"Nothing." By the look of her stubborn chin, Sara wasn't accepting that. "Antsy, I guess. I haven't heard from Karen in a long time."

"I thought you were talking to God about that."

"I was. Am." He summoned a dry smile. "I talk a good line, but I guess I'm not that hot at walking my talk."

"Don't say that. You're one of many people I've met who actually lives his faith. Anyway, who am I to complain? I question everything." She sat down on the chair he held out, set her cup in front of her. She searched out his gaze and held it. "I've been trying what you said, reading the Bible and waiting for God."

Even if he'd wanted to, and he didn't, Cade couldn't help reaching out and gathering her hand into his.

"I'm so glad." He meant it. "How's it going?"

"Not as easily as I'd hoped. Sometimes I think I feel something but others—" she shook her head "—not so much."

"But you can't base faith on feelings. Faith means believing even when you can't see." His heart sang for the huge step she'd taken. But when Sara glanced at their hands still entwined, Cade realized he'd held on too long. He patted her fingers awkwardly and let go. "You'll get there. The important thing is not to give up. By the way, I noticed this in the paper this afternoon."

He spread out the notice he'd torn from the newspaper and smoothed it on the table for Sara to see.

"That is who you were talking about, isn't it? Gideon Glen?"

She nodded slowly, scanning the article and the picture of the elderly gent.

"He's here? In Denver?"

"He's a visiting artist at the university, doing a workshop, it says."

"If only I'd known," she whispered sadly, her face crumbling as she finished reading. "I could have signed up for it. He never gives classes in L.A."

"Maybe you can still get in."

Sara shook her head, pointed.

"It says they're taking only current students and anyway, all the positions are filled." She laid her hands in her lap, lifted her gaze from the article. "Thanks for showing me, though."

Impotence suffused Cade. He wanted to help her so badly, but showing her the article had only brought pain.

Leon chose that moment to light the birthday candles and they gathered with the others to watch Aimée blow them out, her pale face flushed and glowing when her husband kissed her in front of everyone. She opened each gift carefully as if she was storing up memories. Standing to one side of Sara allowed Cade to see the way her brown eyes softened when Leon slid his arm around Aimée's shoulder as she thanked everyone for making her day a special one. After that the guests mingled, but one by one, eventually said their goodbyes.

Judging by Sara's constant reference to the wall clock, she wanted to leave, too.

"Ready to go?"

"Yes, thanks." She threw him a grateful look, then led the way to Aimée. Ten minutes later they were outside, walking toward the car.

He helped her inside the vehicle, wishing he'd warmed it up first. But Sara didn't look cold. In fact, snuggled into her white cashmere wrap, she seemed entranced by the frosted trees along the avenue.

"Isn't it lovely?" she murmured, leaning forward to peer through the clear patch on the windshield.

She was the lovely one, almost ethereal in the shrouded streetlight that added to the misty glow of the car's blue-green dash lights.

"We used to have this video when I was a kid. It was about Jack Frost and how he dipped his paintbrush into the frost bucket and decorated everything. Doesn't it look like he just flew past?" she asked, head turned toward him.

"Uh-huh." Cade felt the tightrope of awareness stretch between them. It was up to him to keep things neutral, but suddenly he didn't want to. He wanted to share this magical evening. One evening. "Are you in a rush to get home?"

"No." She drew two pins from her hair and the entire mass of curls dropped to her shoulders. "That feels better. Why?"

"I want to show you something. Okay?" Cade waited for

her nod before pulling out from his parking space and heading for the hills. He pushed in a Michael W. Smith CD.

"Perfect." Sara leaned back in her seat, apparently content to study the view without conversation.

That suited Cade. His insides were twisted in knots and he wasn't sure he could put two sentences together. Better to remain silent and let her think he was an idiot than to open his mouth and prove he was.

The snaking switchback up the side of the mountain wasn't smooth and after a few snowfalls would be almost impassable, but Cade kept going because now that he'd come this far, he couldn't turn around. He needed the solace of his special place.

But by the time the car tires scrunched through the shale bits littering the area, he'd begun to question this idea. Sara wasn't saying anything. He turned and saw her staring in front of the car's hood, her expression rapt.

"It's beautiful," she whispered a long time later when she leaned back in her seat and studied him. "How did you find this place?"

"Driving around." He shrugged. "I come here sometimes to think. It's quiet and I can sort out my mind."

"Is something bothering you tonight, Cade?" Sara's always-quiet voice fell even softer in the night, a hint of curiosity feathering through it.

"I should have told you the whole truth." He touched her cheek, pulled his hand away. "I come here often after visiting Leon and Aimée."

"Why?"

He shouldn't have brought her here, shouldn't have chosen her as his confidante. But Cade longed for someone to talk to and Sara always listened.

"Whenever I see them together," he began, watching her

carefully to see how she handled his confession. He paused, loath to admit the truth.

"Go on."

"I'm jealous of him, of them, of what they have." The words stumbled over themselves in the rush to emerge. "I know it's wrong and I have no right to feel like that, but times like tonight, seeing them standing together in the doorway, waving at us—I want to be him. I'm jealous of my best friend."

"You're in love with Aimée?" she asked, her tone dubious.

Cade blinked, then laughed.

"No. Of course not. I'm not in love with anyone." Why had he opened his mouth—to her, of all people? "Ignore me, Sara. I'm babbling."

Her blond head waggled back and forth in the spear of moonlight that flooded over her.

"I don't think so." She slid her hand into his and squeezed. "I think you're finally letting the macho tough cowboy rest. I think the real Cade Porter is showing."

"Yeah, well, he shouldn't be." He liked holding her hand. Her skin was silky and warm and provided the connection he yearned for. "Cade Porter has no business wanting what he can't have."

"And you can't have love like Aimée and Leon's? Why?" No condemnation lay hidden in her questions, only a question lurking in the darkness of her eyes.

"I told you. I explained about my desire to follow God's will. God's plan for me is to remain single."

"Yes, you did. Listen, Cade." Sara drew her hand from his and leaned back in her seat, her brow furrowed. "I don't know if I'm the right person to commiserate with you. I've never been in love and I don't want to be."

"Why not?" he asked while his brain said, "What a waste."

Sara glared at him.

"You think I'm too young, that I don't know how precious love is. You're wrong. I do know. But I see Reese when he doesn't know anyone's watching. I see how his world has collapsed around him." Sara squeezed her eyes closed. "He's like a prisoner of the past. It's about all he can do to be both mother and father to his boys while he tries to figure out how to get through the next minute, hour and week." She shook her head vehemently. "I don't ever want to be that dependent on someone else."

"Did you ever ask Reese if he feels he's lost his independence?"

"No. I want him to forget the past."

"Sara—" Cade touched her chin, tipped it up so he could see into her stormy eyes. "She was his wife. He's not going to forget her or what they shared, particularly not with those two little reminders in the house."

"I'm glad he has the twins. They force him to keep going. But—" she dashed a tear from her cheek and sniffed "—to see him burying himself in work, it's as if he's missing a part of himself."

"I know Reese would tell you his wife was the best part of himself and I'm positive he wouldn't trade the time they had together for anything," Cade said softly. "It hurts now, but there's no way he'd want his independence back. He'd be less of a man if he hadn't met her, married her, had children with her."

"That's what everyone says." She accepted his handkerchief, blew her nose and dredged up a watery smile. "And maybe it's true. I don't know. I only know I don't want to ever rely on someone like that. But I won't have to. I'll be too busy with my career."

"So you're willing to give up both your family and love for

a job?" Cade was positive she didn't understand what she was saying.

"It's not just a job. It's a chance to prove I have the talent, the ability, the inner spirit to make my dream come true."

"Prove to whom? Yourself? Or your family?"

"Both."

"And what if you never achieve that dream, Sara? What if one day you wake up and realize that you will never achieve it, that you're all alone? Will it be worth it?"

Sara stared at him for a long time. The words she finally spoke were not what Cade expected her to say.

"Why does God want to deny you the one thing you truly want? Explain that to me, Cade."

"I—I don't know if I can." He licked his lips, dredged up the answers that had never truly satisfied. "Maybe God, knowing the future as He does, is trying to protect me. Maybe I'd make a lousy husband and father."

"I don't believe that. I've seen you with my grandmother, the twins and the kids in the play. I've heard you talk about your sister. You're not the kind of man who treats people he cares about poorly. If I had any doubts, your mega-involvement in Karen's wedding plans would have shown me otherwise a long time ago."

"Am I bugging you with my constant visits?" He watched her face, half wishing she wasn't always so honest.

"Yes. You have confidence in my abilities with the play. You don't show up all the time and question every decision I make there. Why don't you trust me the same way with this wedding?"

"I need it to be perfect." He didn't have any other answer.

"Because Karen's wedding is a substitute for your own?" She nodded when he opened his mouth to refute that. "Woodwards does weddings, Cade. Perfect weddings. We're famous for that. It might not be exactly the way you dreamed it, but it would be wonderful for Karen. Why isn't that enough for you?"

Sara was right. He had been pouring himself into these plans, far beyond what his free time should have allowed, because he knew it would have to last him forever.

"It's not only the wedding, though."

He blinked, frowned at her. Something else was coming and he was pretty sure he wasn't going to like it, either.

"You took sunflowers to my grandmother's house when you found out how much she loves them. You introduced Katie to that guy from your church. You've even got my mother thinking about adding to the rose garden at my parents' because my dad told you how much he loves growing them."

"So?"

"You even spoke to the family on my behalf and asked them to back off throwing us together." Sara laid her hand against his cheek and held it there, her smile wistful. "For which I thank you."

"I wanted to help."

"I know. Like you helped Lisa and Olivia, Reese, the twins and everyone else you meet who's needy. You love people, Cade. You can't honestly believe you don't have a God-given talent for ministering to everyone." Sara pushed an unruly lock off his forehead, then withdrew her hand. "You can't believe, in your heart of hearts, that God would give you such a gift and then want you to turn your back on it."

"Now you're trying to marry *me* off?" he asked, only half joking. "Anyway, it's hardly everyone." He ducked his head to hide his embarrassment.

"Okay, there are the some people you haven't met yet, but I'm positive you'll get around to helping them eventually."

She giggled when he rolled his eyes. "You've helped me a lot, too. I feel as if I finally understand God as I never did before."

"Why didn't you?" he asked, hoping to change the subject.

"Wrong thinking." She threaded her fingers together, then dragged them apart, her smile wistful. "I got sidetracked, thought it was all about me, what I want. It's not. I realize that now. It's all about God and how I relate to Him. I'll be working that out for a while."

"Nothing wrong with that."

"I guess." She tilted her head back, met his gaze. "I know you're far more adult in your Christian life than I am, and I'm aware of my presumption when I say this, but I think you're doing some wrong thinking, too, Cade Porter."

"Do you?" He wished now that he'd taken her for coffee or driven her straight home. Anything but come to this isolated spot where he couldn't get away from her soul-searching scrutiny.

"I messed up on a lot of things to do with God, but one thing I got right, thanks to my grandfather."

"I thought he died after your father was born?"

"Yes," Sara agreed. "But remember the diaries? He came to this country to be a toymaker. His parents owned a pottery factory and they wanted him to continue in their business."

"Right." Where was she going with this?

"Grandpa wanted to make toys. Dolls, actually. They thought he was a fool, crazy to give up their safe, sane world for who knew what in America. Especially because they'd survived the Depression and the war and were into better times. If he'd stayed, my grandfather had his future ready-made."

Cade reached out to switch on the motor, but Sara stopped his hand.

"You'll scare the deer away," she murmured, pointing. In front of them a doe and her fawn were munching on the last of the summer grass. "Am I boring you?"

"Of course not. Continue."

"Well, anyway, Grandfather died before he got his dream, but in his diary he recorded prayer meetings he had with a nameless friend. They both had dreams and they both believed God wanted them to pursue their dreams." She smiled at him. "I'm getting to the point, I promise."

"I'm listening."

"Grandfather affirmed one thing over and over in his diary. That God had created him, known him from before he was born. That He'd planted a desire and a longing in his heart to do that which he loved. To quote my grandfather, 'God doesn't give us glorious dreams only to destroy them. He gifts each of us uniquely and He expects us to use what He has blessed us with to enrich life, for ourselves and others.'"

Sara's face shone. Cade thought he could watch her forever.

"My grandmother would tell you how she clung to that tenet after his death as she prayed for something to do that would allow her to stay at home and raise her son."

"She made wedding gowns." He'd read part of that story somewhere.

"She started by adjusting her own wedding gown for a friend. She built her empire on her own wedding gown. But I digress."

Rats. He'd hoped she'd forgotten what they'd been discussing.

"As I learn more about God, I'm realizing how my thinking about God has been so wrong."

Cade did not want to continue this conversation. It would only fuel his own doubts and he'd resolved not to do that. But he could hardly shut down Sara now that she'd finally begun to rebuild her spiritual relationship.

"I've begun to realize that He isn't a last-minute, throw-it-together God. Everything He created has a purpose and a function and a place in the world. Including you."

Cade shifted, but Sara held his gaze with her intent brown eyes and forced him to listen, the fervor in her voice holding him in place.

"I don't believe God has led you on the path He has, equipped you to raise your sister after your parents died, given you a heart for kids, only to tell you to turn your back on those feelings. God created your giving heart for a reason, Cade."

"You think you know the reason."

"Me?" Sara grinned. "It doesn't matter. It's what you think. Anyway I shouldn't say any more and you're welcome to tell me to mind my own business if I'm way off-base." She suddenly sobered, her eyes solemn as she studied him. "But when I see you with your boys' group, the kids in the play, I know how great you'd be with a family of your own."

"That doesn't always matter, Sara. Remember Leon? Sometimes what we want the most is what God asks us to relinquish."

"Maybe. I think Leon's reconsidered, too. Aimée said they've been discussing adopting a child because they believe God wants them to share the love they can offer."

Cade looked at the clock. "I should get you home now. You have to work tomorrow."

"Yes, I do." Sara studied him intently. "We have four weddings next week. Three of them right after Thanksgiving. It's going to be hectic."

"Let me know if I can help," he said, steering the car back onto the road and down the hill. "Is there anything I need to work on for Karen's wedding?"

"Not yet. I'm almost ready for you to approve the invitations. They'll be printed on a rush order. The flowers are still up in the air, but I've got a couple of ideas. Everything else is pretty well set. You did talk to Leon about catering?"

"Sorry." Cade winced at her glare. "I forgot. I promise I'll do it this week, but I can almost guarantee he'll say yes." He saw her shoulders shake and knew exactly what she was about to say. "Almost isn't good enough."

Their voices emerged in unison. Sara giggled.

"You're learning Grandmother's sayings very quickly. Did she say that to you?"

He shook his head, enjoying the way she relaxed with him, lost the tension that usually held her shoulders stiff.

"No. I heard her saying it to your sister and brother. And your dad."

"You did? When?" She turned her curious brown eyes on him and Cade knew he was caught.

"Uh, I happened to stop by the store last week. You were busy, but your mom asked me to have coffee with her. We didn't mean to eavesdrop, but they were out in the hall and—" He made a face to show his apology. "Your mother told me your dad used to feel he could never measure up to Winnie's standards."

"I didn't know that."

"She said he'd decided in his senior year that he wasn't going to stay at Woodwards."

Sara stared at him in disbelief. Cade wished he'd never mentioned the conversation, but it was too late to go back now.

"Winnie always wanted a family dynasty."

"I'm not sure that's true, Sara. Fiona said when your dad went to college, he finally realized that the florist end of the business was his first love. He decided to make his mark in that area and returned to Woodwards on condition that Winifred allow him to set up and manage Woodwards Flowers."

Sara's puzzled stare softened. A faint smile curved her lips.

"Dad loves plants. He gave my mother gardenias after he

first met her because gardenias symbolize joy and he wanted joy in his life forever. He's such a romantic."

"Each person in your family has a unique history. That's what ties you all together."

"Except me," Sara murmured, her smile fading. "I'm the oddball."

Cade pulled up to her parents' house, switched off the motor. He turned to face her and spoke exactly what he'd been thinking.

"I don't think you're the oddball, Sara. I think you're the bird of paradise, the triumphant showy bloom that makes the bouquet of your family stand out. Being part of Weddings by Woodwards isn't what defines them any more than it does you." He touched a wisp of gold that had curled itself against his headrest. "You are your own person, with your own hopes and dreams. Put your trust in God to work it all out and then rest in His love."

Sara didn't try to break the connection between them. Instead her velvet eyes held his for timeless moments until finally a watery smile lit up her face.

"You're a very nice man, Cade Porter. Thank you for being my friend." She leaned across the gearshift and pressed her lips against his cheek in a fleeting kiss. "Good night."

Then she was gone, out the door, up the walk and inside the house before he could respond.

As he backed out of the drive, Cade wondered what she would have done if he'd turned his head enough to meet her lips with his.

You made a commitment to God. Honor that.

That was his head laying out the facts.

She's a beautiful woman who draws you in, makes you imagine what life could be like. Is that wrong?

That was his heart, spilling out the truth he tried so hard to suppress.

All the way home the battle raged in his mind. Was Sara

right? Was he misreading God's will? But he'd prayed, been certain of his answer.

When Cade pulled into his yard, he didn't go inside the house. Instead he walked around to the back where the soft hum of the hot tub's circulating motor offered a soothing background for his prayer.

"I want to do Your will," he prayed, staring into the stars. "But every day my feelings for her are growing. Please help me. Show me Your way."

He prayed the same prayer over and over as the moon skidded across the sky, then left to make way for the first creeping fingers of dawn. When sunrise flooded the ranch, Cade had no more answers than he'd begun with. Chilled and confused, he went inside to put on the coffee and check his e-mail.

Karen had sent a message.

Everything's fine. Hopefully can get home and marry before New Year's. Lotsa love. K.

Cade opened the front door and surveyed the ranch he called home.

"Will I be this lonely for the rest of my life, Father?"

He could find no answer in the soft mist climbing up the valley.

Chapter Nine

"Is everyone all right with their masks and makeup?" Olivia asked.

Sara scanned the actors' faces, a rush of satisfaction surging through her at the work she'd done. If the play failed, it wouldn't be because she hadn't done her job. A camera flash made her twist around. Cade stood behind her, snapping pictures left and right.

"Okay, one more run-through, guys. Then we're done," Olivia promised. "Thanksgiving's only two days away, remember, so do this well and you can all leave early. We'll hold two more full rehearsals next week before our big night on Sunday." She clapped her hands. "Places, please."

Sara stepped out of the melee and took a seat in the audience. She pulled a notebook from her pocket and as the play progressed, scribbled notes to herself, adding a few extra squiggles when Cade's shoulder rubbed hers as he sank down beside her.

"Hi." *Get a grip on yourself, Sara. Concentrate on the job.*

Cade didn't say anything until the twins emerged from the wings with their costumes askew, followed by their new nanny.

"Um, are they supposed to look like that?"

As his peppermint-scented breath washed over her, Sara felt a quickening in her spirit. She read her senses the riot act. Cade was not eligible. After a minute she reminded herself that neither was she!

"Sara?"

"I see it. They're filling in. I'll fix them later." Surely he could tell she didn't want to talk.

But either Cade was ignoring her unspoken signals or he didn't care because he did not remain silent.

"Is your cell phone off?"

"Yes." She frowned at him for a moment, decided to be blunt. "I can't talk to you right now, Cade. I'm making my final notes." She turned back toward the stage in time to see a mask land on the floor. Thankfully it didn't break.

"I just came from Woodwards. There's a woman there who insists she must speak to you about her wedding."

"I can't right now. One of the others will have to help her." Sara scribbled a note to deepen Lisa's makeup so it would show up better under the glaring lights.

"She'll speak only to you."

Frustrated by his refusal to wait, Sara heaved a sigh and turned to face him.

"Look, I can't run to Woodwards right now. I'm in the middle of something and besides, it's my day off. I'm sure Katie will make an appointment for this person."

"She did," he said, his eyes dark and inscrutable.

"So what's the problem?"

"The appointment for your meeting is in half an hour."

Sara groaned. Another case of having her life run by her family's demands. But that wasn't Cade's fault. She pinched her lips together and nodded.

"You'll be there?"

"I might be a couple of minutes late, but I'll come, yes. Okay?" She waited just long enough for his nod, then hunched forward, her focus on the play.

At least that's what Sara hoped it looked like. But while her eyes followed the actors' progress, her mind was busy wondering what Cade had been doing at Weddings by Woodwards when he knew perfectly well that she wouldn't be there.

Her uneasy feelings burgeoned when he touched her arm and said he was leaving.

"I'll see you later at the store. I want to talk to you about something."

By the time rehearsal was over, Sara had very few legible notes and almost none of her thumbnail left.

"You look upset. Is something wrong with the costumes?"

"No, Olivia." Sara smiled, hoping to erase the concerned look on the other woman's face. She suddenly realized how little she knew about Olivia or the reason she so seldom laughed. "A few tweaks, but I'll take care of those. We're in good shape."

"I noticed Cade left in a hurry. Is anything wrong between you?"

Sara realized that Olivia was under the same delusion her family was.

"Cade and I aren't involved," she assured the other woman. "We're friends and I'm working on his sister's wedding, but other than that—" She shrugged.

"But the way you look at each other," Olivia said, then stopped. "Sorry. It's none of my business. You'll be here Sunday evening?"

"Of course. This production is going to wake up people. Kudos to you for getting this off the ground, Olivia."

"I've had a lot of help. Especially from you." Olivia

hugged her, then stepped back. "I'd better get backstage and make sure everything's put away properly."

"See you Sunday." Sara left a few minutes later and headed for Woodwards. She tried a soothing CD, a boring talk show and silence, but none of them made a dent in her growing trepidation about Cade and their upcoming conversation.

At Woodwards, everyone seemed in a rush. Katie was missing, but Fiona and Cade were deep in conversation at the far end of the reception desk. Their chat ended the moment Fiona saw Sara. Her mother rushed forward and embraced her, which amplified Sara's misgivings.

"Darling! This is Heather Holmes. She wants to speak to you." Fiona drew forward a tall, thin girl who awkwardly thrust out one hand.

"Hello," she whispered.

"Hello, Heather. I'm sorry I kept you waiting. Shall we find some privacy?" Sara cast a backward glance at her mother, who didn't budge from her position next to Cade. "I think Room Six should be free."

"No, it's busy." Her mother smiled. "Try Room One."

The Ivory Room, as Sara had long ago designated Room One, was usually reserved for Woodwards' special clients, those who wouldn't tolerate anything but tea in fine china and sumptuous seating. If Heather Holmes was one of those clients, shouldn't her mother be handling the case?

"Please have a seat. Would you like coffee, tea or soda?"

"No, nothing." Heather shifted restlessly for a moment, then finally met her gaze. "I need your help." She lifted the peacock-blue silk scarf from her neck to reveal a crisscrossed mass of scars. "My mother knows Lisa's mom. I saw what you did for Lisa. I want to know if you can make these disappear, so I can wear the wedding gown I've dreamed about."

"I see." Sara studied the marks. "They're not new," she murmured, praying she wouldn't embarrass the poor girl.

"I was in a car accident a few years ago." Heather gulped. "My fiancé says he doesn't care about the scars, but I care. I want everything to be perfect for my wedding. I can't set a date because, well—" She stopped, licked her lips. Her huge soulful eyes begged Sara for help. "I hate them," she burst out.

Sara touched her fingers, her heart breaking for the young girl.

Please, God, You've got to help. What do I say to her?

"I'm sure it was awful, but you can't hate yourself for something you had no control over," Sara soothed. "A terrible thing happened to you and you have scars from it. Not just here." She touched one of the bubbled ridges with a fingertip. "But also in your heart and your mind. But that isn't the whole story."

Heather stopped sniffing and frowned at her. "It isn't?"

"Hardly." Sara smiled at her. "You survived. You healed. You're moving on to a wonderful future with a man you love, aren't you?"

"I want to. But the marks are so hideous." Her fingers curled into the silken scarf. "I have to keep them covered or people stare."

"You were in an accident. That's not a reason to hide them. But if you're uncomfortable, you can do things to make them less noticeable."

"Like what? More plastic surgery? Then I'll have to wait ages to get married." Desperation shone in the girl's eyes. "Cade said you'd help me."

Cade had a part in this? Nice to know he had faith in her.

A warm little spring of joy bubbled up inside Sara's heart. She'd prayed and God had answered. *Help me now.*

"Let's try something, Heather."

They spent two and a half hours together, but when Sara finally opened the door, rather than tired, she felt exhilarated.

"Come back tomorrow and we'll run over it one more time, just to make sure you're confident."

Heather frowned.

"But won't I have to come back more than that?"

"Well, the technique isn't that—"

"We can't plan a wedding in one day."

"A wedding?" Sara tried to hide her surprise. "What date did you have in mind?"

"Christmas Eve." The girl's eyes glowed. "I've wanted to be married on Christmas Eve ever since I was a little girl."

"But—that's only a month away!"

"I know." Heather's eyes shone.

"But—"

"A month's plenty of time, Sara," Fiona broke in. "We'll work it all out. You have a talk with your parents tonight to see if they're agreeable, Heather. Then come back tomorrow and we'll discuss all the details. Okay?"

Sara stood silent as Fiona continued to talk. Her mother held out Heather's coat, slipped it over her shoulders, then walked her to the door, where a cab waited.

"See you tomorrow, dear," she called, waving.

After the cab had pulled away, Fiona spun around, raced over to Sara and threw her arms around her shoulders.

"I can't believe you did that."

"Did what?" Sara stared at the staff who'd gathered in the reception and were grinning at her. "What?" she asked, aiming her question at Cade, who was also smiling. Why was he still here? Or had he left and returned?

"Heather Holmes is a nice kid. A little spoiled maybe, but that's because she's the only daughter of *the* Handleford

Holmes, a local real-estate fellow." Cade looked embarrassed by her father's loud guffaw.

"More like a real-estate tycoon. Holmes is Cade's next-door neighbor. The guy's been trying to buy you out for a while, hasn't he, Cade?"

"You want to sell?" Sara demanded. "You'd give up your family ranch?"

"I've said no so far. But—"

"They have a huge place in the Ozarks. According to local gossip, his daughter has interviewed a couple of dozen bridal companies in New York alone. I can't believe she'd choose Woodwards after one little visit with Sara." Too late, Fiona seemed to realize how that sounded. "I mean, she wants to be married in a month."

Nice save, but to Sara, her mother's comment was yet more evidence that her mother and probably the rest of the family doubted her abilities.

"Heather may yet change her mind," Sara mused as her father ordered the staff to close up shop.

"I doubt it. She looked very happy with what you'd done for her." Her father petted her head as he had when she was ten.

"Yes, she did." Fiona's smile stretched huge.

"Dinner tonight is on me," Thomas insisted, and he wouldn't be denied even though Cade tried to opt out. "Filbert's will have a table for us in ten minutes."

"I'm not dressed—" Sara glanced down at her jeans and faded blue sweater.

"I need to talk to you." Cade's low insistent voice sounded right behind her. "Now."

"Dinner's a good idea, Thomas. We'll all brainstorm something wonderful for Heather, while Cade tells Sara what we've decided to do for flowers for Karen's wedding." Fiona grabbed her husband's arm and drew him toward the closet where they stored their coats. "Come on, people."

"Karen's flowers?" Confusion filled Sara at the look of guilt flooding Cade's face. "But I thought you agreed with my selections." Tension crept up her back and rested in the tightening line across her shoulders when he didn't meet her stare. "Didn't you?"

Cade glanced at the interested listeners and shook his head.

"Wait," he murmured softly. "I can explain."

"Let's go, folks." Her father shepherded everyone out the door and locked it behind them while her mother surged ahead, dictating directions to Katie and Reese.

Sara was profoundly aware of Cade walking beside her, although he said nothing. Neither did she. She was still reeling from his decision to override her plans without telling her about it. When her father caught up and began asking Cade about his friendship with Heather's father, Sara slowed down, desperate to make sense of what she hoped, prayed, wasn't happening.

"That was quite a coup for you, Sara." Abby, their jewelry designer, loped along beside her, her pretty face clearly visible now that she wasn't wearing her thick jewelry-designing glasses. "Your parents are very impressed. When Cade brought Heather in, your mom couldn't get her to even smile."

"She's shy." Sara couldn't tear her eyes from the back of Cade's head, the straight line of his shoulders, the long stride even her father had trouble matching.

"Is something wrong?" Abby asked as they waited to enter the restaurant.

"I think I'm about to find out," Sara told her as her mother insisted she take the seat next to Cade. Sara turned to the only One she could. *Please, let me be wrong.*

* * *

"I'm so glad you happened to be driving past, Winifred. You'll tell Cade I'm right about the roses, won't you?"

If he'd had a piece of tape, Cade would have used it to gag the lovely Fiona. As it was, he fumed silently. Didn't the woman have any tact when it came to her daughter?

"I need to talk to you," he murmured to Sara, wishing he could have found a way to do this privately.

"Mother purposely placed us in this corner so we could be together. I'd say this is going to be your best opportunity of the evening." Sara dredged up one of those fake smiles she used, the ones that didn't reach her eyes. "Go ahead and talk."

Cade inhaled. This wasn't going to be easy.

"I stopped by Woodwards this morning to drop off that catalog you'd lent me. Your father was showing me some new roses he got in for the wedding on Friday. He was ecstatic. You know how he goes on. Anyway, your mother overheard our discussion about the meanings of different colors of roses. She said white roses are known as bride's roses and mixed with red ones, which are the color of love—"

He was losing Sara and he knew it.

"I began thinking about how Karen used to love it when Trent picked her wild roses in the summer and I thought maybe roses would be a better choice."

"You didn't think that perhaps, because we'd already discussed flowers, I'd considered roses and obviously not chosen them in favor of the freesias and lavender Karen clearly indicated in that album you showed me." Her voice squeaked out tight and angry.

"But your mother said—"

"I'm fine with roses, if that's what you'd prefer, Cade. In fact, I'll have Karen's file on my mother's desk before tomorrow morning. I'm sure she's far better equipped to help you plan your sister's wedding than I'll ever be."

"No! I'm only—"

She jerked her arm from his touch, rose, set her napkin on the table edge with precise care. She dropped her voice so low he had to lean in to hear.

"I tried to tell you to get someone else at the very beginning. But you said you had confidence in me. Enough confidence in my ability to send me Heather for makeup, apparently, but not enough to trust me with all of Karen's wedding."

"Sara!'

She stepped away from him. "I'm sorry, I have a headache. Good night."

Sara kept her face expressionless as she left quickly and without fuss, which meant no one noticed her absence until the server asked for Cade's order.

"Where's Sara?" her mother demanded.

"She's not feeling well. If you'll excuse me, I'll check on her."

"Aren't they the cutest couple?" Fiona whispered behind his back.

Fuming, Cade hurried out of the restaurant and around to the back of Weddings by Woodwards where Sara usually parked her car. He found no sign of her. He drove past her parents' house, but her car wasn't there. Neither was it at the theater where they'd been practicing. Or any of the other places he could think of.

Finally, Cade drove home, irritation ramping up.

What right did she have to be mad at him? He was the client. He was paying the bills. Why shouldn't he choose roses if he wanted to? He knew his sister better than anyone, and Karen loved roses. He pulled into his driveway and stomped the brake to stop the car, irritated by Sara's performance. Why did she have to be so stubborn?

A plain brown box sat on the doorstep. Cade picked it up

and carried it inside, dropped it on the table. After doffing his coat, he opened it and dragged out the contents.

Cade's anger died.

Inside the box sat a creamy white binder, edged in delicate lace trim. Two words had been printed on the front in an elegant scrawl. *Karen's Wedding.* He lifted it out.

Inside the binder, reams of notes spilled from one page to the next. Details he hadn't even begun to consider. Prices for everything. Sample fabrics for tablecloths, napkins, centerpiece ideas. Even thank-you cards tailored specifically to this bride and groom.

And there, halfway through the book, he saw Sara's notes on flowers.

Karen loves lavender mixed with freesias, she'd written. *It was part of her mother's bouquet.*

Cade winced. How could he have forgotten?

Sara had included snapshots of unusual bouquets that someone had obviously arranged for her. Her father? Cade suddenly recalled Thomas trying to get his wife's attention when she'd been talking about roses.

The corner of something stuck out from behind the photo. He tugged one corner. A cream parchment envelope with the Weddings by Woodwards logo on it came loose. Cade opened it.

Dear Karen:
All these things will show you how much thought and time your brother put into making every detail of your wedding perfect. You're very lucky to have someone who loves you so much he puts your feelings first.

Shame suffused Cade in a tidal wave.

Sara had told him her family had overridden bridal plans

she'd made in the past. He'd overheard their meddling for himself. He'd seen how badly she longed to be accepted for who she was.

And what had he done?

Consulted her? Asked her thoughts on changing what she'd put so much effort into simply because her mother made him think she knew better?

No. He'd discarded Sara's hard work and plans as if they didn't matter. As if they were worthless. It wasn't about which flowers Karen had and Cade knew it. It was about his stupidity.

He'd told her he was her friend. That she could count on him. And when she had, he'd let her down. Hardly the actions of a friend.

But Sara was his best friend. She'd become his ally, his confidante, his closest companion. Cade woke up wondering what she was doing, checked in with her at least twice a day simply to hear her voice. He made excuses to visit the store to feel the vital connection of belonging somewhere, to someone. He sought her out partly for the pleasure of sharing her big boisterous family, but mostly because with Sara he felt alive, needed. Necessary.

Sara touched his soul. Cade couldn't bear to see her fight her battles alone. He'd encouraged and supported her whenever possible, hoping she'd let him share her happy and sad times. She made him feel as if he were vital to her life. He'd wanted her to know he would always be there.

By siding with her mother he'd broken her trust.

Now she thought she was truly alone. The oddball. On the outside.

"It's no wonder you don't want me to get married, God," he muttered, glaring at himself in the hall mirror. "What woman would put up with such a dunce?"

Cade closed the binder. Lifted it to put it back in the box.

Something was paper clipped to the back cover. He turned the book over, read a blush-tinted note.

Cade wants everything perfect. Don't make mistakes. Be ready to change.

He tried to imagine those words coming from either Fiona or Winifred's mouths and couldn't. But Sara was more than willing to step back, to let her mother take over. Why?

Because her interest isn't in herself, or even in Wood-wards. She wants the best wedding for Karen. As she wanted the best for Lisa. As she did for Heather.

Cade thought he was the teacher on faith, considered Sara his pupil. He talked a lot about trust, but when it came to action, it had taken Fiona five minutes to start him doubting Sara's choices, just as her family did.

Cade packed everything back into the box and took it out to his car. He didn't care how long it took, he was going to find Sara and apologize for his lack of faith in her.

His cell phone rang.

"Sara?" he whispered.

"She quit," Winifred said.

Hope fizzled.

"Can you believe that? She's quitting when she's just landed the biggest wedding of the year. You have to find her, Cade. Talk her into staying."

Time to choose sides. Cade had no problem. He would always be on Sara's side.

"Mrs. Woodward. I can't talk Sara into anything and I wouldn't want to. I'm supposed to be her friend, but today I let her down badly. I should never have questioned her judgment. And neither should you," he added, struggling to keep the anger from his voice.

"How dare you?"

"I dare because I care about your granddaughter and I see

how much her family's lack of faith hurts her." He had no business saying this, but he was going to do it anyway. "A young girl spoke with Sara for a few hours and trusted her with an entire wedding. Yet Sara's own family questions every decision she makes. Can you imagine how that makes her feel?"

"Sara's very capable, but sometimes her ideas aren't quite appropriate. Fiona told me about those flowers for your sister. Freesias and lavender—"

"Are what my mother carried at her wedding," Cade told her quietly. "Karen wanted the same. Sara understood that. Her choices are client-focused and utterly appropriate. That's why the young girls seek her out. Sara is honest and direct with them. She doesn't care about tradition or fashion. She's on their side and they know it."

"You're saying what exactly?"

"I'm saying that when Sara leaves Weddings by Woodwards, you're going to notice her absence."

"I don't want her to go. She's needed there."

"Needed? Isn't this more about control, Mrs. Woodward?" Cade inhaled, then said what he should have said weeks ago. "Maybe it's time for you to tell her the real truth about why you conspired to get Sara back at work in your wedding company."

"What do you mean?" The laugh held a wobble of nervousness.

"Your granddaughter thinks you want her home because you and the rest of her family don't support her dream, a dream she longs to fulfill. She thinks you believe she isn't capable of achieving that dream. It's hard to argue with her conclusion when you, her family, sandbag her all the time."

"We love Sara."

"Some love. You think up ways to force her into doing your will. You refuse to be the wind beneath her sails and not one of you encourages her to reach her full potential doing the things she loves." Cade dropped his voice. "Could it be that you don't want Sara to leave Woodwards because you know you'll lose a vital, enriching part of the family? Or is it that you don't want her to succeed because you are afraid her success will supersede yours?"

An angry silence was his only response.

"Goodbye, Mrs. Woodward." Cade clicked the phone closed before he could say anything more. He had enough regrets.

The phone rang again but he ignored it, started his car, did up his seat belt and then closed his eyes.

"Where are you, Sara?"

No glimmer of thought enlightened him, so Cade turned to his closest companion for help.

"Lord, I've been an idiot. I need to tell Sara that. Please help me." He kept his eyes closed, waiting for his Father to respond.

The wind—it was the wind, wasn't it?—raged strong and furious across the land. Suddenly a thunk and shudder from his car made Cade open his eyes. A branch from the old maple tree lay across his trunk. He got out to remove it and noticed a flicker of light peeking through the row of spruce trees that led to his grandmother's studio.

Sara.

"Thank you," he whispered.

Without a second thought, Cade switched off the car, zipped his coat and began walking while he pulled on his gloves. Questions of doubt plagued him. Would she even listen to him or had he ruined everything between them?

Cade prayed all the way up the hill.

"Okay, Lord. Help me." He grasped the door handle and stepped inside.

Chapter Ten

Sara didn't hear the door open, but she felt a rush of air swirl past her and into the building. She didn't turn, didn't budge from her perch on the balcony. She didn't need to because she knew it was Cade.

"Sara?" His fingers touched her shoulder.

She jerked away, kept her back to him.

"I'm sorry. I was wrong and I'm very sorry."

It should have felt good to hear that admission, but her heartache didn't ease.

"I know it's glib and too easy, but I mean every word. I am sorry I didn't have enough faith in you to withstand your mother's suggestions." He sat down beside her on the wooden bench, his shoulder bumping hers. "I think I knew I was wrong the moment I did it, but I didn't have enough courage to push back and insist you knew what you were doing."

"So instead you let me look stupid." The long drape of her hair shielded her from Cade's scrutiny and allowed Sara to speak truth. "I thought you were my friend. I thought you were telling the truth when you said you liked what I'd planned for Karen."

"I was. I do! But—" He stopped, drew her curls behind her ear, then tilted her chin so she had to meet his gaze. "I let your mother overpower me."

"Oh, come on." Despite everything, Sara liked his touch against her skin. The warmth of his fingertips made her feel cherished. Which was really a stupid thing to admit when the man had betrayed her. "My mother is half your size."

"So are piranhas."

"That's not nice."

"Not strictly accurate, either. She's more like a barracuda." Cade paused a moment as if waiting for her to agree. "I mean, she's absolutely certain she's right and tenaciously intent on proving it. Like this."

His fingers gripped her arm to illustrate his point. Sara yelped and freed herself, but she couldn't stifle her laughter. Cade Porter had the uncanny knack of drawing women out no matter if they were eight or eighty. She'd seen him make her grandmother's day when he'd returned her glance with a smile that bypassed any younger woman around her. Goodness, he could make *her* feel precious with nothing more than his lopsided grin.

Tonight his leather jacket emphasized shoulders broad enough for the most demanding woman to rest her weary head. And Sara was weary. She wanted nothing more than to relax and enjoy the casual arm he flopped around her shoulders.

"Sara, you know nobody can withstand your mother," he murmured.

The smile lighting his blue eyes glowed electric, zapping a current straight to her heart, coaxing her forgiveness. His cool smile washed over her like a soft spring rain, cleansing her of the pain she'd felt earlier.

"Say you'll pardon me?" he begged earnestly.

"Yes," she agreed, snagged in the promise his eyes offered. "I forgive you."

Cade closed his eyes. He heaved a breath of relief and shifted his arm, hugging her close against his side.

"I don't deserve it, but thank you, Sara." He pressed his lips against her cheek just as Sara turned her head.

Their lips met and for Sara the world stood still. Even Cade seemed frozen, but only for a second. Then he was kissing her and Sara was returning it exactly as she'd envisioned in the dreams she'd told to no one.

After a few moments, she drew away from him. Cade seemed stunned. He frowned at her.

"Should I apologize for kissing you, Cade?" Sara rested her head against him, studying the night sky spread in front of them like a diamond-studded cape while her heart rate slowed.

"It was my fault. I shouldn't have done that."

"*You* didn't. *We* did. Sometimes friends do." That kiss had not been a kiss of friendship and Sara knew it. But she couldn't bear any awkwardness to tarnish the beautiful moment. Later she'd ask herself some hard questions, but now she just wanted to enjoy being with him. "I can't believe it's almost Thanksgiving. What do you have planned for the holiday?"

He shifted beside her, sharing his warmth. Several moments elapsed before he answered her question.

"A turkey shoot."

"A what?" Sara peered at him suspiciously. "You're joking."

"Nope. My boys' group is tomorrow night. I promised them a turkey shoot." He brushed a finger down her nose. "What a disapproving look you have, Sara."

"You can't have children out here, shooting turkeys," she

spluttered. His face split in a huge grin. She thunked his shoulder. "Tease. Explain, please."

"They shoot at a plastic target, with little stick-on darts. Closest to the bull's-eye wins a turkey. You win a turkey, you move on to another game." The moonlight against Cade's chiseled profile emphasized the planes of his tanned forehead.

"You're giving them a chance to win a turkey?" Dubious didn't begin to cover what she was feeling. "Why turkeys and not, say, CDs?"

"I want to make sure each of those kids has some food in the house for Thanksgiving. A turkey shoot was the only thing I could think of. Most of them are awfully proud. If they thought they were taking handouts, they wouldn't accept anything." He shrugged. "But if it's a game and they can swagger home to Mom or Dad and show off what they won, that's a whole other story. We've got a bunch of different stations where they can win other stuff, but most of it is meant for Thanksgiving."

Sara tilted her head back and studied him.

"What?" he asked, frowning.

"You are a very nice man, Cade Porter," she said with sincerity.

He actually blushed before shifting away to face her, legs crossed in front.

"Yeah, well. I want to talk to you about something else, Sara."

"Uh-oh. That sounds ominous."

"Not ominous, but I wanted to ask why you didn't stick up for yourself tonight. You ran away like you'd done something wrong. You let my actions and your mother's control you." His face reflected his puzzled tone. "I'd like to understand why, Sara."

Whatever she'd expected, it wasn't this. She bit her lip.

"What did you think I'd do? It's humiliating when someone overrides your decisions without even telling you. I was ashamed and embarrassed." And hurt.

"I know. Because you surrendered your power."

"I didn't surrender anything. Cade, you saw how they are." She glared at him. "They treat me like I'm five."

"Because you let them." His blue eyes met hers, deadly serious. "Start showing them you're not going to accept their behavior. Show them you're a responsible, able coworker who knows exactly what she's doing."

"It's not that easy."

"Who said life is easy?" He held up his fist and pretended to give her a right cross. "Aren't you the one who's done all the work? Aren't you in charge of Karen's wedding? Don't you know more about what she wants than anyone else at Woodwards?"

"Yes." She batted away his hand and dared him to deny it. Cade smiled.

"You're confident that the choices you've made for her are right?"

"Of course I am."

"Then why didn't you say that? I hired you. I asked you to handle it." His stare would not relent. "You are in charge, Sara. You should have told your mother that you had things well in control and ignored whatever she said. Then you should have hauled me out of there and told me off for not consulting you before I spoke with her."

"What?" She couldn't believe Cade had just said that.

"I'm serious," he said. "I was way out of line."

Dumbfounded, Sara could only stare.

"When you took Heather into that room, your mother didn't stop you, didn't advise you to use green eye shadow or whatever," he said, turning up his palms. "What would you have done if she had?"

"Found a way to get her out of there," she shot back. Then she shrugged. "But Mom never bothers me when I'm doing makeup."

"Did you ever wonder why?" he asked quietly.

She blinked, frowned then shook her head.

"I'll tell you why. I think it's because when the subject is makeup or props for the play, you project an air of authority that nobody questions. You speak more firmly. You say exactly what you need to say." He smiled at her disbelief. "Heather recognized that. So did Lisa. But you don't act like that with your family. What I want to know is why?"

Cade was never satisfied with regular answers. He was always pushing, probing. This time he was probing too deeply. Sara rose, walked to the far edge of the balcony and studied the darkness beyond.

"Afraid to face the truth, Sara?" The soft question came from behind her right shoulder.

"You seem to have all the answers. Why don't you tell me?"

"I think you're so desperate to feel part of their circle, part of Woodwards, you let them take you for granted."

She whirled around, tapped her forefinger against his chest.

"That's why I left for two years? That's why I've worked so hard to build a new career for myself?" Tears threatened, but Sara refused to shed them. She blinked hard until her vision was clear. "I'm not one of your projects, Cade, so forget the psychobabble."

"You're my friend and I care about you." His arms slid around her waist and he pressed his chin against her hair. "I don't like to see you hurting, Sara. Denying that you want to be part of them is only hurting you more."

"It takes away my power. I know. You said that."

"You can build a strong connection without minimizing yourself to fit in. You can be who you are and still be a 'true' Woodward. But you have to be yourself, the strong capable Sara you are, and you have to be that person all the time. Know what I mean?" His breath tossed the tendrils that grazed her cheek.

"I guess. I love my family," she told him, turning to face him. "I do want to be part of their circle. I want to feel included, as if I matter."

"Then stop being their doormat. State your piece and steer your own course. Stop being Sara, their youngest daughter and baby sister, and be Sara, the woman who knows what she's after and intends to get it." He stepped back.

Sara turned to see what he was doing. He was studying her.

"You like to wear jeans. So wear them. Stop dressing up in Katie's clothes. You're not her. Be who you are. Isn't that what you told Lisa?"

"Yes." A smile wiggled up from a hidden place deep inside. "I've said it before. It bears repeating. You are a very nice man, Cade Porter. That wasn't easy for you, was it?"

"Harder than wrestling a bull." He huffed out his pent-up breath. "But worth it. You're worth it."

"Thank you."

"You're welcome." He grazed her nose with his fist, his eyes fixed on hers. "Be who you are, Sara," he murmured. "You're a beautiful person."

She rose on tiptoe, touched his cheek with her lips.

"Thanks, friend."

"Thank you for being my friend even though I messed up." He drew her inside. "You ready to blow this joint, maybe take a break and watch the stars?"

"That would be perfect."

They walked down the hill together. Every so often Cade

would grab her hand when she slid on the gravel. After the second time Sara didn't bother letting go. Friends could hold hands, couldn't they?

Because the evening was cool, Cade insisted huge mugs of hot chocolate were necessary.

"Take the chaise. Put your feet up," he ordered.

They sat in the darkness, sipped their hot chocolate and talked. About anything. About everything. Being here, with Cade, was relaxing. Sara didn't guard what she said because, though he might challenge her opinion, Cade never made her feel foolish or stupid.

In fact, with Cade, Sara felt cherished. Loved.

She sat frozen in the night as the knowledge burst on her conscious mind with the force of an earthquake.

She was falling in love with a man who was determined never to marry!

Sara had never thought about falling in love. Love meant giving up independence. But Cade made her feel more independent than anyone she'd ever met. She'd never met anyone who, just by being there, made her feel strong and capable. She'd never considered loving Cade. Not until tonight, when he'd shown up to ask her forgiveness.

Sara didn't doubt that it was the beginnings of love nestling down into her heart. She just knew. And with the knowing came a desperate sadness.

Cade did not want a relationship. He'd told her so over and over.

So where had these emotions come from? Had God played a trick on her? Was He teasing her? Was this a test?

"Sara?"

"Yes?" She blinked, found him peering at her with concern.

"Are you okay? We've been out here quite a while."

"I'm fine." She needed to leave, to be alone and think about this discovery. "Perhaps I am cold."

"You go inside. I'm going to add a bit of chemical to the hot tub."

Sara didn't need to be told twice. The wind off the mountains now carried bits of ice that pinged against her skin. Sara wandered into the bathroom, relishing the soft glow inside her heart even as her soul wept for what it could not have.

Cade had told her to be herself. Very well.

She sank down on the side of the tub, closed her eyes and prayed.

"God, I don't know why I feel this way. Cade isn't interested in that kind of friend. He's kind and generous and I don't want to hurt him or offend him. Please help me be strong and not show him how I feel."

Feeling a whole lot better, she stood tall when she heard Cade enter the kitchen. Finally she emerged from the bathroom, desperate to say a short goodbye so she could go home, hide out in her room and think.

In the kitchen Cade was putting the kettle on.

"I thought maybe you'd like some more hot chocolate."

"That's nice of you," she said, summoning a smile. "But I think I'd better leave. The weather's getting ugly and it's been a full day."

"Okay." He watched as she gathered her things, then walked out to the car with her. Snow dust covered the ground. "Is everything okay, Sara? I didn't hurt you with my remarks?"

"No." She smiled to ease his mind. "You've given me some things to think about and I promise I will."

"I appreciate the job you're doing for Karen. I couldn't have chosen anyone better."

"Thanks. I'll see you soon. Good night." Sara stood on tiptoe, brushed her lips against his cheek then quickly climbed into her car. As she drove away, she glanced in her rearview mirror. He stood in the same place, watching. Then she crested the last hill and Cade was hidden from view.

"Oh, God, what am I going to do about him?"

Chapter Eleven

"Sara?" Cade wondered for the tenth time if he should have called. But he was desperate and didn't know what else to do.

"Cade. What's wrong?"

"I know it's last-minute, but I'm hoping you can help me out with the turkey shoot. I've already lost one helper to the flu. Another who was going to be there had to cancel to act as labor coach for his wife." He tried levity. "Very rude of her to time their baby's delivery now, if you ask me."

"Truly discourteous. So you want my help," Sara guessed, a chuckle lurking in the back of her voice. "Won't I be odd girl out in your *boys'* group?"

"No. I've also roped in a couple of friends—Leon and Aimée." He stuffed down his excitement. "Could you make it? Even for a couple of hours? I wouldn't ask you, but I really need your help."

"What time?"

"You'll do it? I mean, I know you've probably spent all day planning Heather's wedding and are worn out—"

"Heather was great. In fact, she asked if I'd see some other girls she knows who want help with their skin problems, not just scars. I'll be pretty busy for the next while."

"Good for you," he said, and meant it.

"It's nice to be wanted. Tell me what time you want me and where."

"My place? In a couple of hours?"

"Done. Anything I can bring?"

"Yourself. That's more than enough." He sniffed, glanced at the stove. "Oh, rats! I've got to go. I think I burned the cake."

Cade dropped the phone and scooted to open the oven door. Thick black smoke poured out, setting off two smoke detectors. He grasped the pan with tongs and hauled it outside to sit on a boulder near the back door where the wind would carry away the smell.

"Lord, why did Mrs. Brown have to hurt her ankle today of all days?"

While waiting for an answer he poured himself a cup of coffee and sat down to nurse his scorched thumb. That wasn't the only question he had for God. But even though Cade had thought and prayed about Sara most of the night, he still wasn't at peace.

The phone rang.

"Cade?" Sara sounded defeated. "If I apologize ahead of time, will you promise not to kill me?"

"You can't make it." Disappointment surged inside.

"Oh, I can, but my grandmother overheard my talking to you, and she's issued an edict insisting the whole family pitch in tonight. As a thank-you for sending us Heather." Sara spoke to someone in an aside that he couldn't hear. "Apparently she's arranging for some kind of lunch for your boys, too. She says you should forget about baking."

Cade squeezed his eyes closed. He loved and appreciated

families more than most men, but envisioning Winifred's autocracy with his boys made him shudder.

"Cade? Are you there?"

"Sara. I'll manage. I know she's been ill and—"

"You tell that boy there's nothing I like better than a turkey shoot. Haven't been to one in years. I might take a turn myself." Winifred's voice faded away.

"You heard?"

"Uh-huh." He bit his lip. "There's no way you can stop her, is there?"

Silence.

"Yeah, that's what I thought. Okay, then. The more the merrier. Things might get rowdy. Warn her that some of these kids are not particularly sweet."

"I'll try."

He gulped, almost afraid to ask. "Uh, Sara?"

"Yes?"

"Your mother?" *Please, God, find an emergency for Fiona.*

"She'll be there."

"Oh." *Aren't You listening, Lord?*

"She rushed out of here a few minutes ago in search of a new pair of jeans." Sara's voice brimmed with smothered laughter. "I've never seen her or Winnie in jeans. Tonight should be interesting. I'll be watching how you handle my bossy family, Cade. So I can take notes."

His own words coming back to haunt him.

"Is there any way you can get here before they descend?" he asked, not caring one whit that he sounded like he was begging. Because he was.

"I'll leave now."

"Thank you." He hung up the phone slowly, shot one look at the ceiling. "Thanks a lot."

Cade had a hunch God was laughing.

By the time the kitchen was returned to its spotless state, Sara's car pulled in. He tied up the brimming garbage bag and dumped it in the can before hurrying toward her.

"I'm so glad you're here," he said, and meant it. "I have most of the stations set up, but I wanted to hang a few decorations before the boys arrive."

"Lead on," she said, a dimple flashing at the corner of her mouth. She looked great in her jeans and orange knit sweater. Relaxed even.

"I'm using the riding barn."

"Lots of room. Oh, wait." She touched his arm, then quickly dropped her hand. "You should know, Reese wants to help, too. He's bringing the twins."

Cade gulped. The twins combined with his boys, Winifred and Fiona spelled trouble with a capital *T*. Nothing was turning out the way he'd planned.

"You look like you need to sit down, Cade."

He felt like it, too.

But Cade prided himself on dealing with life's punches. He'd survived a lot. He would not be downed by a few Woodwards.

"I'm—" He stopped, cleared his throat to lose the squeak. "I'm fine. Let's start inflating those balloons."

Sara caught on to his ideas quickly, suggested a few minor changes and added some new touches of her own which boosted the festive air. With most of the decorations in place, they'd barely finished hanging a turkey piñata from the rafters when Cade heard his name.

He looked at Sara. "Winifred."

"Uh-huh. You go tell her where we are. I'll finish the bull's-eye."

"Coward."

"Absolutely." She grinned gleefully as she continued rolling orange crepe paper into curls that went around the target.

Cade trudged toward the house, picking up his pace when he saw a diminutive figure in cotton denim pants and a warm jacket being helped out of an SUV by Reese. The twins in the back let out a squeal when they saw him.

"Hello." He donned his best host smile, then struggled to retain it as Reese began removing cartons and stacking them on the ground. "Um, what is all this?"

"A few snacks for the children. Some board games that might come in handy. Etcetera." Winifred looked and sounded like a queen as she tossed him a stern look that said she hadn't forgotten what he'd said on the phone the other night. She picked up two of the boxes. "My granddaughter thinks this is a worthy cause. I love my granddaughter, so I will help however I can."

"If you're sure you feel up to it," he hinted, watching her face.

"I'm very well today, thank you for asking." Winifred's glare dared him to say any more on the matter.

The battle lines were drawn.

"Then I'm happy to have your help." Cade lifted the boxes from her arms. "Please let Reese and I carry these. The riding barn is right over there. Sara's inside. Perhaps you can help her."

"Certainly." Winifred plunged forward with determination.

The twins dragged at his legs.

"Hey, guys. How are you?" He listened for a moment before explaining about the evening ahead of them.

"A party?" Brett's grin flashed.

"Yep. But we're the hosts, which means we have to make everyone feel welcome and make sure nobody gets left out. It's an awful big job," he said, delighting in their happy little faces. "Do you think you'll like it?"

"You mean, we don't have to shoot anything?" Brady frowned darkly.

"No. That's just pretend."

"I don't like shooting."

"We won't be. You go that way, remember?"

"I know. Sh," Brady ordered Brett as he grabbed his hand and led the way. "Remember the rules."

Cade opened his mouth to tell him the horses weren't around, but on second thought he quickly shut it. No point in ruining a good thing.

By the time he and Reese were loaded with boxes, Aimée and Leon had arrived and were hauling out the prizes Cade had ordered earlier in the week. They all trooped to the riding barn and unloaded.

"Looks like you didn't need us," Leon grumbled after Winifred suggested a new arrangement for the prizes he'd just displayed.

"Don't even think about going, buddy. This shindig was half your idea."

"Incoming." Sara sailed past and winked.

"Perhaps you two gentlemen wouldn't mind humoring an old woman."

"How can we help?" Cade asked, ignoring Sara's smirk.

"If you moved the tables with the juice over here, we'd have more free area for games. Don't you think?" Winifred batted her eyelashes at him.

He would have argued, but she was right.

And so it went for the next hour. Winifred directed and they did her bidding.

"Why don't you stand up for yourself, Cade?" Sara's big brown innocent eyes dared him during one lull. "Be who you really are. Tell her that you have your own plans and you intend on following them."

"Yeah. Why don't you?" Aimée chimed in with a giggle.

"Oh, shut up," he mumbled.

"Daddy, Cade said *'shut up.'* That's a bad word." Brett scowled at him. "It's a rule, Cade. You're supposed to follow the rules."

"I'm sure Cade's very sorry." Reese turned away, shoulders shaking.

Exactly what he needed, more Woodwards on his case. Cade stomped away, grumbling to himself as he moved the bales he'd so carefully arranged this morning while Winifred bossed him unmercifully.

"You'll have to speak up, Cade. My hearing isn't what it was."

"Just praying for help, Mrs. Woodward."

"I think that's been answered. Fiona's here."

Cade held his breath as Fiona burst through the door. He thought she'd be wearing some outrageous designer duds, but wherever she'd found her jeans, she'd chosen well. She fit into the theme perfectly and had even subdued her mass of red curls into a plain, yet elegant, style that didn't compel the usual attention.

Fiona hugged him before she urged Thomas to retrieve a second box of fat round pumpkins that had little lights inside. She and the twins barely finished placing them around the room before the bus with the boys pulled up.

Cade gazed around the space, delighted by the changes his impromptu helpers had created. It looked far better than he'd even imagined.

"Aren't you going to greet them?" Winifred quirked one eyebrow as if to remind him that he was the host.

"Certainly." Cade asked Aimée to write name tags as he welcomed each boy and introduced them to the group. The boys were clearly awestruck and hung around with hands shoved in their pockets until Brett and Brady knocked over the pot of giant sunflowers.

Everyone burst out laughing and the fun began. Sara chose the fishing pond as her station. She looked even tinier in front of the big watering trough Cade had asked his hands to bring in and fill early that morning. The little trinkets he'd purchased had been weighted with stones and wrapped with netting because Sara thought catching them should be more challenging.

Cade couldn't help watching her, charmed by her ready giggle as she teased and laughed with the kids. Her big chocolate eyes shone with happiness. When the twins decided to help, she designated them fishing pond helpers and kept them busy, even though they splashed her repeatedly in their exuberance.

"Five stations was a good idea," Leon told him. "Nobody is left alone and it keeps the boys moving."

"Clearly they're all most interested in the turkey shoot, though." Cade frowned as the first contestant missed his third and final shot. "That's no good."

Thomas, Sara's father, had offered to be the turkey-shooting coordinator. He called a conference.

"That kid is out of tries according to your rules, Cade. And he hasn't won a turkey. Now what am I supposed to do?"

His rules were starting to annoy even him.

"How about calling this the practice round?" Sara whispered from behind them. "That way Dad can let them all have time to get used to throwing the darts."

"Good idea." Cade announced the change. He bumped shoulders with Sara off and on throughout the rest of the evening and enjoyed every encounter.

Two hours later, the games were over and everyone was happily devouring the lunch Winifred provided—steamy hot dogs with all the fixings, chips and soda. Cute little cupcakes with Thanksgiving decorations made a perfect dessert.

Cade waited until the boys were finished eating, then chose a spot between two brothers and began to talk about the meaning of Thanksgiving.

"So you see it's not just the Pilgrims who had something to thank God for. We do, too. We have a great country where we can go to school, eat hot dogs and gather together without anybody hurting us. Those are just some of the things God does for us and for which we should be grateful. But especially because God loves us."

He checked to be sure the twins weren't going to interrupt the next part. Brady was curled up in Reese's arms, fast asleep. But Brett sat on Sara's knee, his eyes alert. Sara, too, seemed caught up by his words. He ignored his stomach's twitch of nervousness.

"God is our Father. For some of us, He's the only father we have. He loves us even more than an earthly father can. He wants us pay attention to what He has to say, to obey those who are in charge of us, to follow His rules for living, like we've been talking about every week."

Cade continued on, honing in on the questions they'd discussed each week. But even as he spoke he recognized that ignoring Sara was impossible. He was constantly aware of her steady stare, her presence.

Later he'd ask himself some hard questions about his reactions, but for now Cade finished his talk, then opened the floor to the boys' usual flurry of questions. Hesitant at first because of the strangers present, they soon barraged him with everything from how God knew what they were thinking to whether a mother's boyfriend was a parent who had to be obeyed.

Some of the questions needed delicate answers. It surprised Cade when Winifred chimed in with a sensitive answer to one of those. His jaw dropped as she engaged them with suggestions pertinent to situations he hadn't expected her to know anything about. Clearly Winifred was more than a canny businesswoman. Her answers reflected a deep living faith.

With only a half hour left before the boys' transportation returned, Cade ended the session with a prayer. Then he asked everyone to put on their jackets. Even Sara's face displayed curiosity when he ushered them outside.

"Join me in a celebration of thanks to our Father, God." He gave the prearranged signal for his foreman to ignite the first rocket. A boom ricocheted across the valley and the night sky blazed with a thousand glimmers. The young faces lit up in pure delight.

"You've outdone yourself tonight, Cade." Sara moved beside him, her arms wrapped around Brett, who was staring into the sky. "Fireworks are the perfect ending."

"Thanks. I don't think this evening would have been nearly as successful without your family, though," he admitted. "They made the difference. Your parents are amazing with kids. And your grandmother—wow."

"She is pretty remarkable." Sara smiled at him, sharing the moment.

How perfect would it be to spend the rest of his life with Sara?

That thought expanded and filled his mind with such longing that Cade got lost in it and only came back to earth at the sound of clapping. He blinked. They were all watching him, grinning.

He bowed at the waist.

"Glad you enjoyed the show. Happy Thanksgiving."

They chanted it back at him as the bus arrived. The kids hurried inside to gather their trophies of the evening and emerged, swaggering with pride.

"See you next week, guys," he said as they climbed inside the vehicle.

Then they were gone. Sara sighed.

"It was a great evening, Cade, but I guess I'd better pack this one up," she murmured, her face tender as she peered down at Brett's sleeping face. "He wanted so badly to stay awake until the end."

"Let me take him." Cade gathered the body into his arms, catching her scent as he relieved her of the precious weight.

Her face was inches from his.

Sara didn't say a word. Cade couldn't. All he could do was stare into her dark soulful eyes while his heart whispered its longing.

"Time to go home." Winifred's voice echoed toward them, shattering the moment.

"I'll get Reese's car keys." Sara turned and raced toward the building. She paused at the door to glance back at him, then disappeared inside.

For a moment Cade was alone, left to appreciate the weight of the small boy sleeping in his arms. Again the yearning ballooned inside and rushed up to choke the air from his throat.

If only—

"Quite a night, young man." Thomas walked toward him, holding up a set of keys. He clicked the fob to start the engine as they walked together toward Reese's car.

"Yes, it was. Thanks to the Woodwards."

"Our pleasure. Anytime you want some help with your group, you let me know." Thomas smiled at Brett's sleeping face. "I've got to get in practice for these grandsons of mine. Won't be long before they're the same age."

"I appreciate the offer, sir. The twins are great kids."

"They grow up too fast. I haven't been spending enough time with them. That's got to change." Thomas eased Brett into his car seat and fastened the harness. He brushed a hank of unruly hair off the boy's face and replaced it with a kiss. Then he straightened. "Kids are a father's biggest blessing, Cade. I think you'll make a great dad one day."

I wish.

"Thanks," was all Cade could say. A shaft of pain speared through his heart. It wasn't Thomas's fault. He couldn't know fatherhood would never happen for him.

Cade turned, caught Sara studying him, a soft wistful look on her face. She blinked and quickly looked away.

"Here's another one, Dad," she said, her voice slightly hoarse. She handed over Brady, then turned and hurried back to the building.

Cade followed Sara, knowing Thomas would stay with the twins until Reese arrived. He found Winifred busily directing removal of the decorations. Aimée and Leon were ordered to carry the empty plastic boxes out to the cars.

"You don't have to do that, folks."

"Many hands make light work." Winifred handed him a paper plate with three cupcakes. "You can have a midnight snack," she said, her pink-tinted lips turning up in a smile. "But don't eat too much. I expect you to arrive hungry so you can make a big dent in that gigantic turkey I'm cooking tomorrow. I hate leftovers."

"Leftovers. Um—" Cade frowned, confused.

"What Grandmother means is, would you please share our Thanksgiving dinner?" Sara translated with a glance of censure at Winifred.

"Oh, no. I'm sure you want your family around you," he began.

"Our family is whoever we invite into our homes. At least, that's how I hope they feel. You come," Winifred ordered. She nodded at Reese. "I'm ready to go."

"So am I." Reese held her coat, waited while she slid her

arms inside. "Thanks for a fun evening. The kids loved it, too. See you tomorrow, Cade."

"But—" Cade knew he should refuse the invitation. Yet he wanted to go, yearned to be part of their joyous family celebration. Was that wrong?

"Come early," Fiona told him, tugging on her own jacket. "Winifred insists we play a game of tag football before eating. It seems to be the only way to get the twins to sit still for the meal. Or most of it."

"You're sure?"

"Young man, a Woodward is always sure. I've already asked Leon and Aimée." Winifred smiled at the couple, then walked up to Cade. She stood on tiptoe, pressed her lips against his cheek. "You did good work here tonight, son," she murmured just below his ear.

Then she left with Fiona on one side, Reese on the other. Aimée and Leon bid him good-night, then followed the others.

Cade stepped outside, watched them wave one last time before they pulled away. He was very conscious of Sara by his side, her face puzzled.

"Winifred didn't look very sick, did she? In fact, she seems to have made a very swift recovery since I've come home."

"Maybe what she needed was a break from business to get back her zip."

Sara faced him, her forehead furrowed.

"Then why not take it? Why involve me?" She gazed into the night sky, hugging her arms around herself as she breathed in the scent of pine filling the air. "It's almost as if she deliberately planned for me to come home."

Cade had kept his suspicions to himself and would continue to do so. "Can I ask you something?"

"Why not?" Sara shrugged.

"Is it really okay for me to go tomorrow? I won't be intruding?" She shivered, so he dropped an arm around her shoulders and walked toward her car. "Tell the truth."

"The truth is my grandmother wouldn't have asked if she didn't want you there." She faced him, moonlight cascading over her perfect features. "Do you have other plans?"

He shook his head.

"Then come. Join us."

"Okay," he said, touched by her simple sincerity. "What can I bring?"

"Not cake," she teased. Her face sobered. "Bring yourself. That's who we really want to see, Cade."

He turned up her collar around her ears, rested his hands against her neck.

"How do I say thank-you for tonight?"

Sara said nothing, her eyes steady on his face. Inside him the yearning built to a crescendo that would not be denied. He had to ask.

"Sara, would it be okay for a friend to kiss another friend— as a thank-you?"

"I think it would be all right, this one time," she whispered, so faintly he had to lean in to hear.

Sara pushed her hands out of her sleeves where she'd hidden them and lifted her arms to circle his neck. Cade's heart hit double time, his pulse hammered in his ears. He slid his hands forward to cup her face. Then slowly, savoring every moment, he tipped his head and touched his lips against hers in a delicate brush, meaning only to graze them before he drew away.

But Sara's long slim fingers urged him closer as she kissed him back. When she finally stepped away, Cade's world spun like a kaleidoscope, leaving him with two certainties.

That kiss had been a mistake.

And he wanted to repeat it.

"Thanks, friend." He eased her arms from his neck and set her free. He opened her car door, helped her inside then closed it and silently watched until she disappeared from sight.

Then he let the truth in.

He cared for Sara, more deeply than he'd ever cared for any woman before. He couldn't imagine what it would be like not to see her each day, to watch her in his grandmother's studio, to share silent meaningful looks with her, to watch her eyes dance when she teased him.

The truth was, he couldn't imagine his life without her.

But he'd made a promise.

Not my will but Thine be done.

"Tomorrow," Cade begged, staring at the dusting of stars crowning the dark and distant peaks. "Give me one last day with her. Please?"

He waited, breathless in the silent beauty of the night.

"One day, then I'll give her up."

He took the single shooting star as an affirmation that God agreed.

Cade closed up the riding barn, sampled one of Winifred's cupcakes and soaked in the hot tub until the wee hours. The entire time he prayed, begging for the Lord of his life to change His mind. To no avail.

In the deepest recesses of his brain, Cade knew the love he'd found could not be acted upon. He'd learned his lesson. Another woman did not have to die for him to understand that God had not chosen marriage for him.

Chapter Twelve

Sara peeked out between the curtains, desperately searching the audience for Cade's handsome face.

"He has to come. He's the reason I got into this thing in the first place. He's on the hospital board. He wouldn't miss Olivia's fund-raiser. Not for anything."

Wouldn't he? She'd said the same thing to herself for the past fifteen days and still remained unconvinced.

Ever since Thanksgiving, Cade had gone out of his way to avoid her. At first she left phone messages, sent e-mails, even tacked notes on his door. If it had to do with Karen's wedding, he relayed his wishes through Katie or her mother, or even Reese. But Sara had not heard a word even though she prayed constantly.

Something was definitely wrong.

"It's time to start, Sara. Is everything all right?" Olivia looked remarkably composed for this debut.

Sara envied that composure. She felt like she was in a barrel tumbling over Niagara Falls; one minute furious that Cade could dump her so easily, bawling her eyes out the next because after Thanksgiving she'd been so sure he felt the same as she had.

"Sara?"

"Everything's ready." She hugged the quiet, solemn woman she'd come to know. "Break a leg."

"Yeah." Olivia grinned and clapped her hands. "Places, please."

Sara risked one more peek. Her heart lifted. Cade was there, sliding into his seat at the last possible moment before the curtain went up. Avoiding her again. How much more obvious did he have to make it that he didn't want to talk to her?

Wincing, she took her place in the props area and ordered her brain to concentrate on the task before her.

"It's not dark enough, Sara. Make my scar really stand out so they'll understand how horrible it is to see it for the first time," Lisa ordered.

Sara complied. For two hours she concentrated on perfecting every detail of her special effects. Suddenly it was the last scene and she was all alone in the room. She sank into a chair, weary beyond belief.

"Thank You for helping me, God."

From out front came the sound of thunderous clapping. Sara didn't move even though she'd promised Olivia she'd be there to take a bow. Eventually the actors brought in their masks, removed their makeup. She congratulated each on their splendid performance, pretending a happiness that didn't quite reach her soul.

"Sara?" Winifred burst through the door, her arm looped through that of an older man. "Darling, that was fantastic!"

Sara opened her mouth, but no words came out. It couldn't be, but the man looked exactly like—

"Darling, I want to introduce you to Gideon Glen. He was a dear friend of your grandfather's. In fact, he and Adam used to pray together three times a week."

Gideon Glen was her grandfather's prayer partner?

"He came to see your play. Gideon, this is my granddaughter, Sara."

The silver-haired old man didn't bother with pleasantries. His gaze went straight to the workbench where Sara had laid the masks. He examined each one, touched them, even turned them over. When Lisa arrived, he beckoned her near and studied her face. Then his gaze slid to Sara. He frowned but said nothing.

"Sara's been talking about working with you for years, Gideon. The hours she spent on this play were endless. It hasn't been easy to replace her in the store, but if the play helps raise money for the hospital, then I'm happy." Winifred's chatter died away when the famous special-effects artist shushed her.

"How long did it take you to build the masks?" he demanded.

"Well, not that long. I started with Lisa, but she couldn't wear a mask because it hurt, so I created some facial effects to enhance her character's changes and—" She was babbling. Sara swallowed. "Several weeks."

He frowned, studied Lisa's face a second time then poked at one of the masks. Sara steeled herself for rejection. She'd been silly to imagine she could ever work with the likes of this creative genius. She was a makeup artist, that's all. An ordinary makeup artist.

"Excuse me," she whispered. "I need to pack up everything."

"Wait." Mr. Glen lined up four masks side by side. "Which of these would you say turned out the best?"

"I like Lisa's makeup but also this mask." She lifted it, touched the nose, the eye sockets.

"Because?" he prompted.

Sara didn't know what to say, didn't understand what answer he sought.

Gideon Glen took the mask, set it down and then grasped her hands. Sara heard a noise at the door but she ignored it, her attention riveted to the man in front of her.

"You have a rare gift, my dear," he said so softly she almost couldn't hear. "You see with your soul. We see what you want us to because you allow your hands to display your heart."

"Thank you."

"It is the truth. Each of your masks is wonderful. As is the makeup. They tell us, without words, exactly what that character is feeling at that moment. Even if it was a black-light performance and we couldn't see their gestures or even hear their voices, we would understand the character because of your work on the faces."

Humbled by his generous words, Sara smiled.

"Thank you again."

"Your grandfather had just such a talent. I've always been sad that the world never got to see the genius of his porcelain faces. The world must see yours. Will you work with me?"

"I—I—"

It was everything Sara had ever dreamed of. It was the goal she'd striven toward, the culmination of years of longing to be recognized as someone unique, an individual who had something of her own to give.

Sara couldn't say a word.

"I understand. You need time to think. To plan." He squeezed her hands, let them go. "I am staying in Denver for two more weeks. Can you see me after my classes? Perhaps we can spend time creating together?"

"I'd like that," she rasped, her heart singing.

He smiled at her, touched her cheek.

"So much of you reminds me of my dear friend. Those eyes, they are Adam's. The chin is the same, a witness to determination. Your grandfather would be very proud of you, my dear."

"Thank you."

"We're all proud of Sara." Her grandmother hugged her.

A moment later the elderly pair left. The room emptied except for Cade, who stood in the doorway.

"Congratulations," he said. Was there an empty hollow ring to his voice? "You've achieved the first step to your dream with Mr. Glen."

"Yes."

Sara couldn't look away, couldn't ignore the etched lines around his eyes that hadn't been there on Thanksgiving. Couldn't stop staring at the tightness of his lips or the hard edge of his jawline that told her he'd lost weight.

"I've heard from Karen. She's coming home. She wants to be married on New Year's Eve." He stopped and when she didn't respond, Cade hurried on. "I understand that you'll be too busy with Mr. Glen now. You'll be going back to L.A. I'm happy for you. Most of the wedding details are taken care of. Katie or someone can handle things. Don't worry about it."

He turned to leave.

"Cade?"

"Yes?"

Sara let her eyes soak in his presence, gloried in the reality of his being here, now.

"I love you."

He blinked, frowned.

"It's true."

"Sara, it's been a big evening for you. The excitement, Mr. Glen—" He stopped, swallowed. "I'm sure you don't mean that."

She'd spent so many years hiding the real Sara, pretending

to be someone else, someone who fit in with other people's plans. But in Cade's absence these past days, she'd searched her soul and turned to God for her true identity.

Suddenly she wasn't interested in pretending to be anyone other than who she was, Sara Woodward, makeup artist, in love with Cade Porter.

"How do you know I don't love you?"

"Because you can't. I can't." He dragged a hand through his hair. "Sara, I told you. I will never marry."

"I didn't ask you to marry. I told you I loved you." She prayed for courage to be who she was, independent, strong, God's child. "I've loved you for a while, Cade. Almost from the beginning, I think. Only I was afraid of love, afraid you'd want me to be someone I'm not. Isn't that ironic?"

"I don't know what you mean."

"Here I am, finally being myself, a woman who is truly, deeply, completely in love with you, and you want me to pretend it isn't true." She tried to smile and couldn't. "You want me to pretend it doesn't matter to me that your sister is coming home and you'll be able to stop worrying about her safety? You want me to pretend that I don't go to sleep at night wondering what I've done to offend you so much that you can't even talk to me on the phone. You want me to be a stranger."

"Sara, this decision—it's not my will. That's the whole thing." He sagged against the wall, his face ragged. "It's God's plan for me and I can't fight it. I won't."

Sara had no explanation for the solid confidence that filled her. She could not explain why she knew it was okay to lay her heart bare even if Cade didn't respond the way she wanted. All she knew was that she'd been praying for weeks for God to give her the confidence, the courage and the faith to be the person He'd created.

There was no going back now.

"You once told me my family didn't treat me the way I wanted because I let them steal my power. You were right, Cade. I was a scared wimp. I felt abandoned. I was afraid I'd never get to do the things I thought were so important and I was determined to prove I didn't need anybody, that I could do everything on my own." She stood tall, faced him down. "That was a lie. I'm not lying to myself anymore, Cade."

"That's good."

"I won't lie to you, either." She walked toward him, stopped when she was mere inches away.

"Sara," he groaned, closing his eyes for a moment when she touched his cheek.

"Listen to me, Cade. Neither you nor my grandmother, nor my parents, nor anyone else can tell me what God has placed in my heart." She dropped her hand but refused to back down. "I know the truth. My feelings aren't some childish whim I'll grow out of. I love you."

"But—you can't!" he spluttered, glaring at her.

"Because you've decided?" She shook her head. "I'm God's child. If He leads me back to L.A., I'll go. If He tells me to stay, I'll be here." With every word Sara felt strength infuse her. "You see, I've finally figured out that my dependence has to be on Him. I have to put my future in His hands. That's exactly where it belongs."

"Which is what I've done."

She stepped back and studied him.

"Really? You've been working your faith a lot longer than I have, Cade, so I don't want to question you. But I have to ask, when you kissed me, were you playacting?"

"No!"

"Then I'll assume you have feelings for me, as I have for you. So I have to ask, why would God give us those feelings?

Does He torture people by giving them desires and then telling them they can't have them?"

"No. I don't know. Yes!" he said explosively.

She shook her head.

"That isn't the way you described God to your boys, Cade, and it isn't the way you talked about Him to me." She ached for him to see God as she finally did. "You said God knows everything about us, every yearning, every desire. So I believe He knows my heart and my feelings."

"Sara—"

She smiled.

"I'm not going to argue or try to persuade you. I'm going to pray and wait to know His decision."

The words flowed out of her in a flood, but even as they dissipated into the air, Sara realized that whatever feelings Cade had locked up inside, he would not act upon them. She admired his resolve even as her heart broke.

How could she have ever thought she could live her life or reach her goals alone?

You brought me home to Denver. You helped me find myself and work that I love. You are my Lord. Please tell me what to do now.

In that instant Sara knew there was nothing more she could do.

"I'll do my best to make Karen's wedding a wonderful occasion," she promised. "Anything you need, I'm here. You only have to call. But I think it would be better if I didn't go out to your ranch until Karen arrives."

His head jerked upward, his lips opened, but Cade said nothing. After a moment he simply nodded.

"Goodbye, Cade," Sara whispered. Then she turned and walked away.

Chapter Thirteen

"Someone to see you, Cade."

Sara!

Cade tore his gaze from the ledger he'd been mindlessly staring at for hours and surged to his feet. He blinked.

"Mrs. Woodward?"

"Cade." Winifred thrust out her hand. "I'm here to check out the site for Karen's wedding. It's something I do for every Woodwards bride. We don't want any surprises on the big day."

"As long as no one comes into the house, it'll be fine," his housekeeper muttered.

"What's wrong with the house?" he demanded.

"What's wrong, he asks." Mrs. Brown beckoned to Winifred. "Take a look at this and tell me if you don't think something should be done." She led the way to the living room.

Cade trailed behind the two women, curious to see the problem.

"Our girl is coming home in a week and this is what she'll see when she arrives." Mrs. Brown flicked a disdainful finger at the sleek red leather. "Nothing but sad memories, if you

ask me. It's not even comfortable," she added, as if that were
the icing on the cake.

"Let's see." Winifred seated herself with great delicacy.
"Oh." She stared at Cade, her eyes narrowed. "Were you
going to keep the door closed?"

"Of course not." Cade glanced around the room and knew in-
stantly that Karen would avoid coming in here. "This used to be
her favorite room," he murmured, wishing he could have those
days back to savor one last time and knowing that was selfish.

"We'll need to rearrange," Winifred murmured.

"No." Sara had done her part to make Karen's wedding
flawless. Now it was time for him to do his. "We'll get rid of
it, all of it. I'll buy something new."

"At last." Relief filled his housekeeper's round face. She
hugged him.

"What do I do with this stuff?" he wondered aloud.

"I have an idea about that."

Arrangements were made. Winifred agreed to meet Cade
at a furniture store in Denver to choose new pieces that would
suit the house style. He arrived at the appointed time, but it
wasn't Winifred who met him at the entrance.

"Hello, Cade. Grandmother isn't feeling well so she sent
me."

Sara's beautiful face was thinner, her eyes no longer
sparkled with that zest for life that he'd noticed at their first
meeting. Cade's anger built.

Ill? He almost snorted. No way. Winifred was up to her
usual manipulations. But for Sara's sake, he smothered his
frustration, kept his face impassive.

"Thank you for helping."

"I want everything about Karen's wedding to be perfect. I
told you that." Sara preceded him inside, but she offered no
opinion as they wandered the aisles.

"Can you please say something?" Cade begged when they reached the other side of the store. "I have no clue about this stuff other than that I don't want that white furry thing or the pink one with gold legs."

"Still not into the froufrou, huh?" She smiled and immediately he relaxed. "What happened to the red leather?"

"Donated to the teens' room at church," he told her.

"They'll love it." Their glances held a moment too long. Sara looked away first. She cleared her throat, kept her chin down.

"Look, just tell me which one you prefer, Sara. I trust your judgment." But he hadn't, Cade realized. He didn't trust Winifred, he didn't trust Sara or himself. In fact, he wasn't sure he trusted God right now, or at least his interpretation of God.

The knowledge gutted Cade, but there was no time to dwell on it.

"What about that sectional? The cream one?" She led the way, pointing out all the features. "You could have this coffee table. It's exactly the right height for a family to sit around and play a game. And those lamps will shed just enough light to read stories by. You could put a side table here…"

The clerk arranged the items as Sara spoke and before long a comfortable, family-style room evolved. It even bore Sara's signature color in the orange corner cushions and flecked the fabric of the big recliner.

"What do you think?" she asked, tilting her head to study his face.

"It looks perfect. I'll take it," Cade said, entranced by the glow that illuminated Sara's gorgeous eyes. "All of it. If you can deliver it tomorrow."

"Certainly." The clerk hurried away.

"You haven't even sat in the chair," Sara murmured. "How do you know—?"

"I just do." To prove it, Cade sank into the velvet seat, stretched out. The hair on his arms stood straight when Sara sat down on the sofa, an arm's-length away. "Thank you for helping me. It's perfect."

And it was. Perfect for a family.

But not his family.

"I hope Karen enjoys it. When does she arrive?" Sara's brown eyes met his, said a thousand things without even moving her lips.

"Hopefully before Christmas," he mumbled while his heart said, *You and I belong together,* and his soul wept. *My heart will always be with you.*

"Then it will be a merry Christmas for both of you," she whispered.

The clerk cleared his voice.

"I'd better go. I've a lot of last-minute details for Heather's wedding." She rose, fiddled with her coat, pulled her orange silk scarf around her neck, her eyes avoiding his.

"Perhaps I'll see you there," he murmured, yearning to ask her to stay a little longer, knowing it would do neither of them any good. "Thank you for this."

"You're welcome." One last faint smile, then she hurried away.

Cade gulped down the rush of loss that swamped him. He rose, completed the transaction and left the store. He wandered down the twinkling street, oblivious to the crowds rushing past. Maybe it had been stupid to buy that furniture because every time he saw those orange cushions, he'd think of Sara.

As if he could forget.

"Hey, Cade." Lisa grabbed his arm, stood on tiptoe and kissed his cheek. "I wanted to say merry Christmas in case I don't see you again. Right after Heather's wedding we're leaving for Hawaii. Do you have your shopping all finished?"

Shopping? He stood dumbfounded as she prattled on, hugged her before she left. His brain finally broke free of the fog. No way would he slump around the house anymore. If this is what God had decided for him, he'd make the best of it. And to do that, he'd give his sister a Christmas she'd never forget. He shoved his hat a little snugger on his head and headed for the huge department store at the end of the street.

To get there he had to sidestep around a tiny girl with shiny blond ringlets. She stood gazing into a jewelry store, transfixed by a small musical box in which what was clearly the sugar plum fairy from *The Nutcracker* ballet pirouetted.

"That's what I want for Christmas, Mommy. Will that be under the tree for me on Christmas morning?"

"You'll have to ask Daddy."

"Ask me what?" A tall, slim man joined the pair, his smile huge. The little girl repeated her request as the man scooped her up in his arms and kissed her rosy cheek. "We'll see, honey. Right now, how about we find some pizza?"

The three joined hands, giggling as they slipped and slid across the street to a pizza place.

That's what I want for Christmas. Sara. A family. Love.

But that was what Cade couldn't have.

Sara signaled the organist then started the first of Heather's bridesmaids down the aisle. Two more followed. The organist caught her signal, changed the tune. Everyone rose.

"You're a beautiful bride, Heather," she whispered. "Now enjoy your wedding."

Heather's radiant smile warmed the icy spot in Sara's heart. Beneath a canopy of fir arches laden with twinkle lights, the girl grasped her father's arm and walked down the aisle toward the man she loved, confident and assured in the gown of her dreams.

"Dearly beloved…"

Sara found Cade watching her. The entire time the minister repeated the age-old vows, his sapphire stare held her like a moonbeam. Although she tried to break the connection, although she heard her grandmother's sibilant whisper in the vestibule behind her, Sara could no more fracture the connection between her and the man she loved any more than she could stop wishing she was the one in the wedding dress.

The first notes of the triumphant processional rang out.

Sara blinked back to reality, to her job. Stuffing away her longings, she snapped back to work as if nothing had happened. Only later, when the bride and groom had departed and the last few guests were bundling up against the Christmas Eve snow did she see Cade. He appeared in the one instant when she was finally alone and handed her a small flat box.

"Merry Christmas, Sara." He touched her cheek with one fingertip then left.

"Merry Christmas, Cade." She glanced at the tiny baby in the manger at the front of the church. "Please be with him."

Chapter Fourteen

Karen arrived at the ranch at 2:00 a.m. on New Year's Eve morning.

As he hugged her, Cade whispered a prayer of thanksgiving. Karen showed him her engagement ring; they drank hot chocolate and chatted for hours. Finally his sister said what was so clearly on her heart.

"Travis and I want to get married today, Cade. Our C.O. arranged for a special license for us. It won't be fancy but—"

He pressed a finger against her lips.

"It will be beautiful, sis," he told her. "I have it all arranged. Here." He handed her the binder Sara had assembled for her. "A very special woman helped me arrange this for you. Read it all the way through and then we'll talk."

In the lonely hours that stretched from Christmas morning until today Cade had fretted, worried, planned and worried some more. He'd also prayed. But he found himself doubting the words of reassurance the pastor offered in last Sunday's message, doubting the very Scriptures he read. He'd planned Christmas around Karen. Her absence had magnified Cade's doubts until he questioned his very understanding of God.

Stressed about whether Karen would arrive in time, if she'd accept the wedding he'd planned, whether Sara would still be around to manage it, and most of all, if she'd already left Denver and returned to L.A., Cade felt doubts creeping in about every aspect of his faith. But now that Karen was home, he shoved them all to the back burner and concentrated on her.

"Cade, you are the best brother." His baby sister wrapped her arms around his neck and bawled all over his shirt.

Cade held her tight as he relished what he knew would be the last few precious moments they'd share alone. Then he dialed Sara's number.

"Karen's home. She wants to get married tonight."

"Really? I'm so happy for you." Sara's voice trembled. She quickly got it under control and became very businesslike. "I'll be there in twenty minutes. Everything's ready to go."

"Good."

Silence stretched between them. Then she said, so softly he almost missed it, "Don't worry, Cade."

"With you in charge, I won't."

Sara arrived and immediately went to work, shooing Karen into a bedroom to try on each of the three gowns she'd brought along as she rattled off orders to Cade and Mrs. Brown. They grinned at each other and complied.

Winifred arrived at ten to personally fit the gown. Reese and Thomas were dispatched to hand-deliver the rush-printed invitations. Fiona alerted the attendants when to arrive, then gathered Woodwards' already-harried staff in Emily's studio to decorate with Thomas, who had the floral arrangements well in hand. Cade notified Aimée and Leon. After that he called together his own staff to arrange sleigh rides for the bride, groom and guests up the hill to the studio.

In the end, everything fell together very simply.

Until Travis showed up around three to pick up Karen and they realized they'd forgotten to tell him the new plan. Forbidden from seeing the bride, who was at Woodwards' salon anyway, he traipsed around the premises with Cade and pronounced himself very happy with the arrangements. He wondered aloud about his apparel.

As usual, Winifred remained in control. She sent Reese with Travis to find appropriate clothing, then rechecked her list. Worried about the elderly woman, Cade insisted she relax and share a cup of coffee with him. Winifred didn't waste the opportunity.

"You do know you're making my granddaughter miserable, don't you?" she shot at him, her porcelain face stern and unyielding. "Do you love Sara, Cade?"

"Of course." He was sick of pretending love hadn't taken over his heart.

"Then why are you pulling away from her?"

Everyone was busy with a job. The house was calm, quiet. That silence was Cade's undoing. He poured out his concerns, worries, fears and deepest longings.

"You believe God doesn't want you to have your heart's desire? But why do you think God would work against what He's created—you?" Winifred frowned, her tone dubious. "Doesn't it make more sense that it's your will and not His that you're following?"

"Why would you say that?" He should have known she wouldn't understand.

"Because I think you made this assumption about God's will for you at a time when you weren't thinking straight. You'd lost your fiancée in a very tragic manner. I'm sure you felt even more abandoned when your sister also had to leave."

"I'm not a child, Winifred. I know what I prayed. I know what the answer was."

"What was it?" She leaned forward. "Give me the details of how you came to this certainty that love and the blessings God gives with it are not for you."

"I—" Cade closed his mouth, thought for a moment. Why had he been so sure? He shuffled through the memories. "Afterward—there wasn't anyone. I mean, I felt frozen inside. I couldn't imagine going through it all again."

"Understandable. But why attribute that to God?" Winnie demanded. "What sign did He give you?"

"I don't remember a sign."

"Then what? Confirmation? Did you lay a fleece before the Lord which he definitively answered, leaving no doubt in your mind that God was against marriage for you?"

"Ah, no, but—"

"Then what?" she snapped.

The pressure and stress of the past weeks suddenly overwhelmed Cade. He lost his temper.

"Because He took my parents and left me alone. I raised Karen alone and when she left, I stayed here and faced every day alone, asking God to give me someone special to share my life with," he blurted. "And I lost her."

Winifred opened her mouth to argue, but he didn't give her the chance.

"When Marnie died, I finally understood what He was trying to show me. I can't get married. I'm scared of it happening again."

"Young man." Winifred tapped his shoulder with her tiny fist. "Do you really think God ended your fiancée's life just to stop you from marrying?"

"Yes." It sounded different when he said it aloud. "Sort of."

Winnifred shook her head.

"Why not?"

"Because God doesn't work like that, Cade. He doesn't

place a yearning in our heart and then tell us, 'Oops, sorry, you can't have that.' That's not the nature of God."

"Then what's your answer?" he demanded angrily.

Winifred grasped his hand, her eyes softening.

"Could it be that you feel guilty?" she murmured. "Perhaps you began to feel somehow responsible, as if you should have, could have, prevented her death. Maybe that guilt subconsciously grew in your mind until you transposed it onto God."

"She's right. Marnie didn't die because of you, Cade." Karen stood in the entry of the kitchen.

"Let's not talk about it." Cade shook his head. "I don't want to spoil your day."

"You'll only spoil it if you let this go on." Karen sat down beside him. "Marnie was sick. We just didn't know how sick."

The details bloomed in his mind with brilliant clarity.

"She had headaches."

"And maybe that should have been a clue, but we didn't know. *You* didn't, couldn't know. *Marnie's* aneurysm was not your fault."

Not guilty? He looked from Karen to Winifred.

"So why did God let her die?"

"You'll never know that, Cade. Not until heaven at least." Winifred patted his shoulder. "Just as you'll never know if you would have actually married if she'd lived. We live by faith, Cade. We trust God because He loves us. Don't you think that God our Father has clear and unmistakable ways to let you know if He thinks you're making a mistake with your life?"

"I never thought of that."

"Because your thinking was confused. It happens when we take our eyes off God and lose our focus. It also happens when we let fear push its way into our hearts."

"Fear?" He wasn't afraid of anything. Except losing Sara.

"Are you sure you haven't let fear in, that it hasn't masqueraded as God's will in your mind?"

"Because you don't want to risk losing someone again?" Karen murmured.

"I don't know. Maybe." His mind was a blur, but Cade knew one thing. He had to understand what God wanted him to do. "So how do I know His will?"

"I think you need to ask Him to show you. And then you need to wait."

"But wait how long?"

Winifred wrapped her knobby fingers around his and squeezed, her smile stretching across her face.

"You wait until He answers, loud and clear. And then you make a decision."

"I can't ask Sara to wait, to put her life on hold while I try to get a grip on mine." Cade shook his head. "I won't."

"Sara's not waiting. She's figuring out her own path, the one God is leading her on." Winifred let go of his hands, leaned back. "I've learned a hard lesson from you, Cade. I cannot manipulate my granddaughter, force her into something, because I want my way. I've hurt her so much because I refused to accept her for all the wonderful things she is. I was a stupid old woman who was afraid she'd lose her granddaughter. Instead I drove her away."

The tears dampening Winifred's cheeks surprised him.

"Sara's not that easily manipulated."

"Thank God. You helped her, Cade, when we, her family, should have. You gave her the courage to be who she is, to be strong enough to push on with her life in spite of our manipulation."

"Are you going to tell her you faked your illness to get her home?"

"Smart man." Winifred smiled. "I've already told her. And

she's forgiven me. I'm not the reason she cries her eyes out every night."

Relieved he hadn't been the only one suffering, Cade listened to Winifred.

"Sara is strong. Strong enough to follow God's leading, to withstand me if she has to. Not a lot of people can do that." She gave a self-deprecating laugh. "Sara has a self-confidence, an assurance that lets her explore who she is. She's learned some fine things from my friend Gideon, and she's not afraid to fail."

"And now she's leaving." The death knell punched straight to his heart.

"Is she? She hasn't said." Winifred shrugged. "All I know is that she's determined to use every talent God gave her and we are behind her one hundred percent."

"She's lucky to have you."

"Nothing to do with luck," Winifred snorted. "It's all part and parcel of God's plan. He's planned for you, too. 'I know the plans I have for you. Plans to prosper you and not to harm you.' It's right there in Proverbs. Stop clinging to the past, Cade. Stop using it like a shield to hide your guilt and your fear. Open your heart and see what God has planned for you today."

"How?" he asked hoarsely.

"Forget yesterday. Concentrate on what God has for you today. If He puts love in your heart, don't you think you should find out what He wants you to do with it?"

"Is everything all right here?" Sara stepped into the room, her eyes moving from Cade to her grandmother to Karen, who was openly weeping. "What's wrong?"

"Not a thing. In fact, I think things are finally going to be right," Karen told her, brushing away her tears. "Isn't it time for me to get married?"

Sara checked her watch, gasped.

"Yes, it is. Grandmother, can you—"

Winifred rose, hugged Sara.

"I can and I will. You're the planner, darling. You go with Karen. Cade and I will make sure everything else is ready." Winifred looped her arm through his. "The Lord is giving us a wonderful way to start this New Year. Let's help everyone enjoy it."

Chapter Fifteen

"The twins?" Cade stood behind Sara, watching Reese and Fiona struggle with red bow ties around the little boys' necks.

"I had to. Karen's ring bearer has the chicken pox and her flower girl is stuck in a blizzard in North Dakota. The twins are a last resort. Do you mind?"

"Not a bit," he said as Olivia moved around the room lighting candles. "I see you roped her in, too."

"Well, she offered to help watch the twins later."

"I'm not criticizing. I wanted this to be an inclusive family event. And it is. Thank you, Sara."

She nodded but said nothing, her brown eyes soft, brimming with—love?

"Can we talk later, after this is over?" he asked.

"Sure."

Behind them a door opened.

"Looks like the bride is ready," Sara whispered. They turned to gaze at Karen, stunning in the white velvet gown she'd chosen. A sassy bit of fake fur nestled in her hair. In her arms she held a sheaf of dark purple lavender and white freesias that filled the room with their fragrance. "Okay?" she asked.

"Perfect," Karen responded. "All I need is my big brother to give me away."

"I'll never give you away. Consider it more of a lifetime loan," Cade said, holding out his arm. "I'm reserving all big-brother rights, though."

"Deal."

Sara fluffed out Karen's short train, straightened Cade's tie, her eyes meeting his as she stood on tiptoe.

"Are you ready?" Sara's whisper was for his ears alone. She wore a dark dress, understated to direct all the attention to the bride, as a good wedding planner would. But around her neck lay a blazing orange stone, the fire opal necklace he'd given her for Christmas.

Cade stared into Sara's eyes and knew he'd never loved anyone as much as he loved Karen's wedding planner. But this wasn't a time for words, so he only nodded.

Once Thomas had the groom and his men at the altar, Sara signaled the organist. She nodded at Reese, who whispered last-minute orders to his sons before sending them down the aisle. Brett flung rose petals all over the place, while Brady carefully marched beside him, clutching the white satin pillow with the rings. The crowd chuckled. Sara breathed a sigh of relief when the twins reached the front.

"Bridesmaids." She urged each of Karen's three friends down the aisle. "Now the bride."

"Wait!" Karen let go of Cade's arm to hug Sara. "Thank you so much," she whispered. "You're the sister I used to pray for."

"You're so welcome." Sara smiled. "Go," she murmured, but Cade saw the mist fill her eyes.

"Thank you from me, too, Sara."

She nodded, pressed a hand against their backs.

Cade's chest swelled with pride as he walked down the aisle. He kissed Karen's cheek.

"Be happy." Then he passed her hand to Trent's. Finally he took his place in the first row beside Aimée and Leon.

The minister, who'd seen Karen through the loss of their parents, her teen years, leaving home and her first deployment, offered a reminder of how well the Lord had guided her steps to this point in her life.

"Tonight you take another leap of faith, knowing that you love each other, trusting God to direct your futures. Marriage is not a step to be taken lightly, but it is to be taken confidently, with the assurance that although you may fail each other, for no one is perfect, your Father, the One who gave His life for you, will never fail you. He is there, overseeing every step. As long as you fix your focus on Him as the center of your relationship, He will see you through every step on the pathway of your lives together."

That was it. That was what he'd been missing.

If he was to blame for anything, Cade now knew he was to blame for expecting too much from whoever came into his life. No one could take the place of Karen, his parents, his past. No one could fill the holes left by years of being alone.

Yet he hadn't been alone. God had been there, right beside him, teaching what Cade had been willing to learn, patiently waiting until he was ready for the next lesson of faith.

Was Sara that next step?

Cade wanted her to be. Love for her was a steady flame in his heart. He couldn't fathom his life in ten years without her. And yet niggling doubts still cluttered the backstage of his brain. What if—the phrase just wouldn't be silenced.

But so what? There was no rush. If God wanted them to be together, it would happen.

A wave of pure calm broke upon Cade's soul as the minister pronounced the couple man and wife. The future wasn't any clearer to him than it had been.

But that was okay. God would work it out.

He needed to tell Sara, to seek her opinion, and listen to her thoughts about the future. But Sara was busy.

Cade told himself to be patient, but as the night wore on and midnight drew nearer, he tracked her down, visually followed her every move until he saw her slip out the balcony doors by herself.

"Okay, Lord. This is it. Help me." He moved across the room, used a side door. Sara stood leaning against the railing, her gaze on the mountains and the black shadow of the timber ridge.

"I will lift up my eyes unto the hills whence cometh my help. My help comes from the Lord who made heaven and earth. He will not allow my foot to slip or to be moved. He who keeps me will not slumber. The One who keeps Israel will neither slumber nor sleep."

Cade recited it from memory, the verses his grandmother had taught him so long ago. How could he have forgotten that promise?

"Cade, I—"

"The Lord is my keeper; the Lord is my shade on my right hand. The sun will not smite me by day, nor the moon by night. The Lord will keep me from all evil, He will keep my life. The Lord will keep my going out and my coming in from this time forth and forevermore."

Cade drew Sara into his arms and gazed upon her lovely face, allowing the peace that passes understanding to wash over him.

"I love you, Sara."

Her breath whooshed out in surprise. Her eyes filled with tears. "I love you, too."

"I'm not sure of our future. You have your goals and I want you to achieve them, even if that means you have to leave here. I need some time to get rid of my preconceptions and listen to what God is telling me. But I am trusting that He brought us together for a reason and I will wait for Him to work out the future. Will you wait, too?"

Sara's fingers slid up his shirtfront, fiddled with his tie. She was silent for a long time, but when he finally pressed her chin upward, she was smiling.

"What's so funny?"

"We are. Here I am with a family who loves me, a legacy I was afraid of and all I could do was run. There you are, wanting a family and a legacy, and in your own way, you were running, too. God must have a lot of patience."

"Does that mean you see our futures somehow together?" he asked, pushing the wispy tendrils from her face.

"I'm not going anywhere, Cade. Working with Mr. Glen helped me realize that no applause, not even an Academy Award, could feed my soul the way helping Lisa and Heather and the other women who've come to me have done. Grandmother has asked me to build a special service at Weddings by Woodwards for brides or grooms who have special needs."

Cade frowned.

"Did she ask before or after you told her you weren't leaving?" he asked darkly.

Sara giggled as she slid her arms around his neck.

"After. Grandmother has confessed all, my darling. And she's promised she'll step back and let us seek God about our next step."

"Sure she will," he jeered, but he smiled. "I love you, Sara. I think I have since the day I met you. I believe God is going to give us our own Rocky Mountain legacy, one we can build on for years to come."

"As long as He's the boss, I'm good with that." She tilted

her head as, inside, the guests began the countdown to a new year. "Are you going to kiss me, Cade?"

"Yes," he promised, waiting until the perfect moment. "Happy New Year, my darling Sara."

Cade kissed her until a sonic boom ripped through the valley and the doors behind them swung open.

"Fireworks," Brett yelled, pushing his way between them.

"Me, too." Brady pulled on Sara's sleeve. "I can't see."

Cade handed her one twin, lifted the other and wrapped his free arm around Sara's waist.

"Cade, this is too much," Karen said, snuggled in her new husband's arms.

"The hands asked if they could do it. And I think it's perfect."

Guests and hosts alike stood watching the display. When it was over, someone led them into *Auld Lang Syne*.

Everyone sang. All, except one small elderly woman who stood to the side.

"I promised I'd leave those two up to You," Winifred Woodward whispered, watching as Cade led Sara out of the night air and into the warmth of the studio. "But I never said anything about Reese."

Her eyes tracked a tiny shooting star as it flew across the southern sky, then winked out just above the brook that divided Cade's property from his neighbor.

"Olivia," she whispered in satisfaction. "I was thinking the same thing."

Winifred rubbed her hands together and moved inside, eager to begin work on a new campaign that had nothing to do with Weddings by Woodwards.

* * * * *

Dear Reader,

Welcome to Weddings by Woodwards, the hottest bridal store in Denver, run by a meddling matriarch and her family. But even in a family that works together, there are problems. Sara Woodward felt her family was the problem, until she realized that family offers a bulwark against the hard knocks, that they can support and encourage if she lets them. I hope you enjoyed the story and I hope you'll come back to Woodwards again soon, to read Reese's story.

Until then, I wish you the blessings and joy of family and friends, of community and support, of love in all its myriad forms, but especially I pray you'll know the love of God, who longs for us to be part of His family.

Blessings,

Lois
Richer

QUESTIONS FOR DISCUSSION

1. Sara left her home and family to pursue a dream, believing her family had never accepted her for who she was. Discuss ways we may hamper our children from being the people God intended them to be.

2. Cade suffered great loss in his life. List the ways loss affects our ability to relate to God and the path He leads us on.

3. Winifred started a business and raised her family as a widow in a foreign environment. Talk about ways we can build and maintain strong, effective lives even in the face of great struggle, and how this affects our families, who look to us for leadership.

4. The twins play a large part in Sara's life back at home. Discuss situations in which children can drive a family apart, and compare them to the ways children can draw a family closer.

5. Sara began by helping one girl, and ended up with a whole new career. What are ways we can look beyond our present circumstances, good or bad, and find the courage to help others? How does ministering to others impact our faith?

6. Fiona, Sara's mother, tried to dissuade Cade from going with the flowers Sara had chosen. Discuss ways to deal with people in your own life who, though well-meaning, often override your own preferences or force you into situations you'd prefer to avoid.

7. Sara longed for love but felt it would hamstring her. She believed going it alone was the only way to achieve her goals. Propose situations in which going it alone is vital to following God's leading.

8. Comment on times when you've isolated yourself and later realized you do not have the support group around you that you need. List the difficulties in reconnecting with others who could assist you on your faith walk.

9. Winifred believed Cade had misunderstood God's will. Do you think this was the case? Think about ways you've found to ensure that you are doing God's will and not your own.

10. Sara learned that in order to be whole, she had to stop pretending, even if that meant she hurt others. Suggest ways in which we all pretend, and the problems that occur because of that.

11. Weddings are one of the most celebrated events in a person's life. Share ways one can prepare oneself and one's children for the demands a marriage will make.

12. The vows made at every wedding are usually a personal choice that reflects the couple's intent for their future together. Organize a list of promises you feel should be included in bridal vows.

Love Inspired
HISTORICAL

*Powerful, engaging stories of romance, adventure
and faith set in the past—when things were simpler
and faith played a major role in everyday lives.*

Turn the page for a sneak preview of
THE MAVERICK PREACHER
by
Victoria Bylin

*Love Inspired Historical—love and faith
throughout the ages*

Mr. Blue looked into her eyes with silent understanding and she wondered if he, too, had struggled with God's ways. The slash of his brow looked tight with worry, and his whiskers were too stubbly to be permanent. Adie thought about his shaving tools and wondered when he'd used them last. Her new boarder would clean up well on the outside, but his heart remained a mystery. She needed to keep it that way. The less she knew about him, the better.

"Good night," she said. "Bessie will check on you in the morning."

"Before you go, I've been wondering…"

"About what?"

"The baby… Who's the mother?"

Adie raised her chin. "I am."

Earlier he'd called her "Miss Clarke" and she hadn't corrected him. The flash in his eyes told her that he'd assumed she'd given birth out of wedlock. Adie resented being judged, but she counted it as the price of protecting Stephen. If Mr. Blue chose to condemn her, so be it. She'd done nothing for which to be ashamed. With their gazes locked, she waited for the criticism that didn't come.

Instead he laced his fingers on top of the Bible. "Children are a gift, all of them."

"I think so, too."

He lightened his tone. "A boy or a girl?"

"A boy."

The man smiled. "He sure can cry. How old is he?"

Adie didn't like the questions at all, but she took pride in her son. "He's three months old." She didn't mention that he'd been born six weeks early. "I hope the crying doesn't disturb you."

"I don't care if it does."

He sounded defiant. She didn't understand. "Most men would be annoyed."

"The crying's better than silence… I know."

Adie didn't want to care about this man, but her heart fluttered against her ribs. What did Joshua Blue know of babies and silence? Had he lost a wife? A child of his own? She wanted to express sympathy but couldn't. If she pried into his life, he'd pry into hers. He'd ask questions and she'd have to hide the truth. *Stephen was born too soon and his mother died. He barely survived. I welcome his cries, every one of them. They mean he's alive.*

With a lump in her throat, she turned to leave. "Good night, Mr. Blue."

"Good night."

A thought struck her and she turned back to his room. "I suppose I should call you Reverend."

He grimaced. "I'd prefer Josh."

* * * * *

Don't miss this deeply moving Love Inspired Historical
story about a man of God who's lost his way
and the woman who helps him rediscover
his faith—and his heart.
THE MAVERICK PREACHER
by Victoria Bylin
available February 2009.

And also look for
THE MARSHAL TAKES A BRIDE
by Renee Ryan,
in which a lawman meets his match in a feisty
schoolteacher with marriage on her mind.

Love Inspired.
HISTORICAL
INSPIRATIONAL HISTORICAL ROMANCE

Adelaide Clark has worked hard to raise her young son on her own, and Boston minister Joshua Blue isn't going to break up her home. As she grows to trust Joshua, Adie sees he's only come to make amends for his past. Yet Joshua's love sparks a hope for the future that Adie thought was long dead—a future with a husband by her side.

Look for
The Maverick Preacher
by
VICTORIA BYLIN

*Available February 2009
wherever books are sold.*

Steeple
Hill®

www.SteepleHill.com

REQUEST YOUR FREE BOOKS!

2 FREE INSPIRATIONAL NOVELS
PLUS 2
FREE
MYSTERY GIFTS

Love Inspired

YES! Please send me 2 FREE Love Inspired® novels and my 2 FREE mystery gifts (gifts are worth about $10). After receiving them, if I don't wish to receive any more books, I can return the shipping statement marked "cancel". If I don't cancel, I will receive 4 brand-new novels every month and be billed just $4.24 per book in the U.S. or $4.74 per book in Canada, plus 25¢ shipping and handling per book and applicable taxes, if any*. That's a savings of over 20% off the cover price! I understand that accepting the 2 free books and gifts places me under no obligation to buy anything. I can always return a shipment and cancel at any time. Even if I never buy another book, the two free books and gifts are mine to keep forever.

113 IDN ERXA 313 IDN ERWX

Name	(PLEASE PRINT)	
Address		Apt. #
City	State/Prov.	Zip/Postal Code

Signature (if under 18, a parent or guardian must sign)

Order online at www.LoveInspiredBooks.com

Or mail to Steeple Hill Reader Service:

IN U.S.A.: P.O. Box 1867, Buffalo, NY 14240-1867
IN CANADA: P.O. Box 609, Fort Erie, Ontario L2A 5X3

Not valid to current subscribers of Love Inspired books.

Want to try two free books from another series?
Call 1-800-873-8635 or visit www.morefreebooks.com

* Terms and prices subject to change without notice. N.Y. residents add applicable sales tax. Canadian residents will be charged applicable provincial taxes and GST. Offer not valid in Quebec. This offer is limited to one order per household. All orders subject to approval. Credit or debit balances in a customer's account(s) may be offset by any other outstanding balance owed by or to the customer. Please allow 4 to 6 weeks for delivery. Offer available while quantities last.

Your Privacy: Steeple Hill Books is committed to protecting your privacy. Our Privacy Policy is available online at www.SteepleHill.com or upon request from the Reader Service. From time to time we make our lists of customers available to reputable third parties who may have a product or service of interest to you. If you would prefer we not share your name and address, please check here. ☐

LIREG08R

TITLES AVAILABLE NEXT MONTH

Don't miss these four stories on sale January 27, 2009.

APPRENTICE FATHER by Irene Hannon
With an orphaned niece and nephew depending on him, commitment-shy Clay Adams calls upon nanny Cate Shepard to save them all. With God's help and her kind, nurturing ways, Cate may be able to ease the children into their new life. And her love could give lone-wolf Clay the forever family he deserves.

THEIR SMALL-TOWN LOVE by Arlene James
Eden, OK

A high school reunion means a trip home for new Christian Ivy Villard…to mend some fences. Past mistakes await her in tiny Eden, Oklahoma—like her former high school sweetheart, Ryan Jeffords. Yet a second chance at love is waiting for them, if they're brave enough to take it.

A COWBOY'S HEART by Brenda Minton
A lot of folks depend on ex-rodeo star Clint Cameron, including his twin four-year-old nephews. So why can't his stubborn neighbor, Willow Michaels, accept a little help with her bull-raising business? Clint's got a lot more than advice to offer Willow, if only she'd look deep in his faithful, loving heart.

BLUEGRASS COURTSHIP by Allie Pleiter
Kentucky Corners

Rebuilding the church's storm-damaged preschool is easy for the celebrity host of TV's *Missionnovation*, Drew Downing. Rebuilding lovely hardware store owner Janet Bishop's faith in God and love may be a bit more challenging. But Drew is just the man for the job.

LICNMBPA0109